Unethical

Unethical

Terrence Brothers

ISBN:	Hardcover	978-1-4257-9369-2
	Softcover	978-1-4257-9347-0

This is a work of fiction. Names, characters, places and incidents either are the product of the author's imagination or are used fictitiously, and any resemblance to any actual persons, living or dead, events, or locales is entirely coincidental.

This book was printed in the United States of America.

To order additional copies of this book, contact:
Xlibris Corporation
1-888-795-4274
www.Xlibris.com
Orders@Xlibris.com
45219

Acknowledgments

I thank God and the few loved ones who've stuck by me.

Chapter 1

On a quiet afternoon in Las Vegas, Billy Brocks allowed himself a chance to relax as he sunk deeper into the black leather recliner in his luxurious office. He's enjoying an extravagant lifestyle as a successful attorney in the Las Vegas Valley.

As he got lost in his thoughts, he was suddenly interrupted by the soft voice of his secretary, Simone, over the intercom. "Mr. Brocks, a client is here to see you. Should I send him in, sir?"

"Who is it, Simone?"

"It's Mr. Cooper, sir."

"Yes, send him in, please."

When the door swung open to Mr. Brocks's office, a tall black man quietly entered, wearing a dark blue Armani suit with a white hat and a pair of white shoes to match. The man's voice filled the room when he saw his attorney slowly approaching him. "You're the man, Mr. Brocks. You know I wouldn't be here if it wasn't for you."

Billy Brocks gave a sly smile as he walked toward the man and shook his hand. "That's right, Charles, you owe me one."

It just happened that Charles Cooper was only one of several clients that Mr. Brocks had managed to have released from the Las Vegas county jail the day before. The well-dressed black man had been caught red-handed while driving around town with a loaded firearm in his possession. He had been pulled over and arrested after a police officer conducted a random search of his vehicle. Charles Cooper had notified Mr. Brocks, and after reviewing the police report, Mr.

Brocks filed a motion in the Clark County Courthouse alleging that the arresting officer had not had probable cause to pull over or search Mr. Cooper's vehicle. The officer involved held Mr. Brocks in high respect, so he admitted to the judge at the time of the hearing that Mr. Cooper had not violated any traffic violations and he had only pulled the vehicle over because his own curiosity had gotten the best of him. The officer said he wondered how a young black man, such as Mr. Cooper, had been able to afford a new-model Mercedes Benz. The district court judge ruled that probable cause in the case did not exist, and Mr. Cooper should not have been pulled over or searched just because he was a black man driving a nice vehicle. The judge ordered that the case be dismissed.

Meanwhile, as the two men stood inside the spacious office, the temperament changed as they both fell silent. Thoughts raced through both of their minds before Mr. Brocks broke the silence. "What's next for you, Charles?"

The large black man continued to gaze aimlessly outside the large window of Mr. Brocks's office before replying, "I don't know, Mr. Brocks. I'm thinking about moving back to LA, but I think my wife and I would stand a better chance of raising our daughter right here in Las Vegas. I still haven't decided yet, but hopefully, I'll figure it out before it's too late."

That was a statement that Billy Brocks could definitely relate to. Although he's an attorney who's living the American Dream, Billy Brocks had not figured things out yet. After a few moments of silence, Charles Cooper thanked Mr. Brocks for all he'd done. He looked his attorney in the eye and gave him a firm handshake before turning to leave. Charles Cooper made his exit from his attorney's office with hopes of never needing the man again.

Several minutes after Charles Cooper had left his office, Billy Brocks was still sitting on the edge of his desk, wondering to himself the same thing he'd asked Mr. Cooper, "What's next for you?" That's a question he'd been asking himself for the past few years, but the answer remained the same. He simply did not know.

Born and raised in Las Vegas on April 18, 1969, Billy Brocks derived from a wealthy Caucasian background. Raised only by his father and grandfather, they were the two men he'd always looked up to. Unfortunately, both men had passed away, but Billy still remembered their deaths as if it had just happened yesterday.

Billy Brocks had never known his mother or grandmother. All he'd ever known was the awful things he'd heard about them through his father and grandfather. Edwin Brocks, Sr., had died of a stroke at the age of seventy. Billy had only been twenty-five at the time and away at law school when his grandfather passed away.

He had only been a few months away from taking his bar exam, so his father decided against telling him about his grandfather's death until he'd finished law school and passed the bar exam.

When spring arrived, the young aspiring attorney returned to the fabulous Las Vegas just to learn that his grandfather had passed away. Billy couldn't believe it, and he could barely hold himself together when he realized he'd never see the wise man alive again. Edwin Brocks, Jr., consoled his son and explained why he'd felt it was best to wait before telling him about his grandfather's death. Both men had been attorneys themselves, but it was the grandfather who'd dreamed of seeing Billy grow up to become a successful attorney. Billy had been the reason why both men had shed blood, sweat, and tears to build Brocks & Brocks Law Offices from the ground up. It's now the most exquisite law firm in Las Vegas, and Billy was finally going to fulfill his grandfather's dream, but it bothered him that the old man would not be around to see it happen.

Edwin Brocks, Jr., was the one who'd taught Billy everything he thought he'd need to know about being a successful attorney. He'd taken Billy to the firm on a daily basis and had shown him the ropes until his own life had suddenly come to an end.

One early Sunday morning, Billy was awakened by the loud ring of the telephone. He'd been reluctant to answer it at first because he was hoping that his dad would answer it. Besides, it was the weekend, and Billy had planned to sleep in. After about the fourth ring, he finally reached over toward the nightstand and grabbed the receiver. "Hello."

"Hi, my name is Lisa Rider, I'm a nurse at Valley Hospital. I'm sorry to disturb you, sir, but we have an Edwin Brocks, Jr., here at the hospital, would you happen to know him?"

"Yes, he's my father. Is he all right?"

The nurse heard the change in Billy's voice after hearing his father's name, so she continued in a caring voice, "I'm sorry, but he's suffering from a rare heart condition, and we're not sure if he's going to make it."

After telling the nurse he'd be there shortly, Billy hung up the phone. He quickly climbed out of the king-size water bed and ran down the hall to his father's bedroom to see if the phone call had been a joke. His thoughts raced rapidly as he ran into the bathroom. His father hadn't been home at all the previous evening, but Billy hadn't realized it until he'd checked the bedroom. He'd known about his father's heart condition, but had never known it to cause his father any problems. Billy didn't know what to think. He flushed the toilet, but didn't bother wiping up the pee that had splashed on the toilet seat. He reached for his face towel and washed his face before brushing his teeth. After rinsing out his mouth and spitting the contents inside the sink, Billy hurried down the hallway toward his bedroom. He wasn't going to work, so he didn't waste time worrying about what color suit or tie he would wear. After slipping into an old pair of sweat pants, a sweatshirt, and a pair of Nike jogging sneakers, Billy grabbed his car keys from the nightstand before heading toward the garage door. It was dark when he entered the garage, but it didn't take long for his eyes to adjust to the darkness. Billy squeezed behind his father's truck before making his way toward the car that was parked at the very end of the four-car garage. He reached the car and quickly snatched off the cover that had been placed over it. He got inside the smoky gray BMW and immediately started the engine before closing the door. After flipping a switch on the sun visor, the garage door began to roll open. As soon as the door had fully opened, Billy stepped on the gas pedal and was already at the tip of the driveway awaiting to enter the street. He flipped the switch again and was on his way up the street when the garage door closed.

Once he'd reached the freeway ramp, Billy turned on the radio as he heavily accelerated the BMW 7 series. He was desperately hoping that his father would pull through, but tried his best not to think about it. He sped up as he recalled the nurse's tone of voice when she said they didn't know if his father would make it. He swerved in and out of traffic as he traveled along the smooth highway and was suddenly relieved when he finally saw the large red sign flashing Valley Hospital. He began to switch lanes in a desperate attempt to make his way toward the highway's exit ramp. Once inside the hospital's parking lot, Billy immediately spotted a parking space large enough to hold the BMW. He stepped out of the Beamer, but didn't worry about locking the door. He simply activated the car's alarm by using the remote control on his key ring before running briskly toward the hospital's entrance. As he advanced closer toward the door, he tried to remember the name of the nurse who'd called his father's house. He couldn't remember, so he entered the building and walked directly to the counter that was closest to the door. An elderly nurse, who worked inside the ICU, was watching as Billy approached the counter; so she quickly stood to help him. "May I help you, sir?" she asked softly.

"Yes, ma'am. I received a call from a nurse who works here—I can't recall her name—but she said that my father, Edwin Brocks, Jr., is here at your hospital and I'm wondering if you could tell me where he is?"

"Hold on a minute, sir. Let me check the roster."

As soon as the elderly nurse reached for the roster behind the counter, another nurse had just walked up to remove a name off it. The two nurses exchanged a few words before the elderly one pointed the younger one in Billy's direction. Billy watched closely as he stood with a concerned look on his face. The younger nurse walked over and shook his hand with a firm grip. "Hi, are you the son of Edwin Brocks?"

"Yes. Is he all right?"

"I'm Lisa Rider, the one who called to inform you of your father's condition. I'm sorry to be the one to tell you this, but your father passed away shortly after you and I talked on the phone."

"What! I don't understand."

"I'm sorry, sir, but he didn't make it."

Billy was sad and confused. He never heard the nurse say she was sorry because he'd passed out and was stretched across the hospital's floor in a supine position. When he opened his eyes shortly afterward, the nurse was cradling his head in her arms and fanning his face with her hand. After fully regaining his consciousness, Billy was suddenly in a hurry to leave the hospital. He'd never expected this to happen again, but since it had, he wasn't sure if he'd be able to deal with it. He had barely been able to cope when his grandfather died, now he was faced with the fact that his father was dead too. Billy no longer had the men to look up to, but he vowed to always remember the words that the two men had always instilled in him. They constantly reminded him that women were never to be trusted. Maybe that explains why neither man had a woman by his side at his time of death.

As Billy sat in his office on the edge of his desk, he was staring down at his own life. He'd reached all the goals that he'd ever set for himself, but he was still unhappy and felt that something was missing. It appeared that he was following in the same footsteps as his father and grandfather, and he wondered if they too were as lonely and unhappy as he.

Chapter 2

"Flight number 171 from Atlanta to Las Vegas will be leaving in approximately ten minutes. I repeat, flight 171 from Atlanta to Las Vegas will be leaving in approximately ten minutes!"

After hearing the announcement come over the intercom, Crystal Tradwell slowly rose to her feet. She'd been sitting in the lobby of the Atlanta airport for at least an hour before they'd finally announced her flight. Crystal immediately found herself regretting that she'd worn her red high-heeled pumps because they'd begun to hurt her feet. She contemplated on changing them before boarding the plane, but quickly decided against it because she doubted that she could get her bag retagged and still make her flight on time. She desperately wanted to get started on her journey, and although she'd never been to Las Vegas, she was extremely anxious to start her new life because Atlanta had given her too many bad memories. She felt that she had been in Georgia for too long as it was and decided that it was time to do something different with her life.

The product of a biracial relationship, Crystal Tradwell was as sexy as they come. Standing at only five feet four inches tall and weighing one hundred and five pounds, her body had all the right curves. Most men were usually confused about her nationality, but still found themselves attracted to her. A lot of women had also been known to drool over Crystal, and although many were jealous, Crystal hadn't allowed that to bother her. Being a mixture of Asian and African American, Crystal's parent's interracial relationship had soured soon after she was born. They'd often used Crystal as an excuse for many of their fights and arguments until the abuse had eventually turned directly toward her. After several of their nosy neighbors had called the police and reported possible child abuse, the State of Georgia had come and removed Crystal from her parents' custody before placing her in foster care. Diagnosed with attention-deficit disorder by the age of five, Crystal was terrible. Paying very little attention to anybody, along with her constant temper tantrums, proved to be too much for anybody to handle; so she bounced around from one group home after another until she'd eventually ran away at the age of fourteen. The Atlanta streets were like an adventure to Crystal. She'd never been loved, nor did she know how to love, but maybe it's something she'd be able to learn with time. It hadn't taken her long at all to realize that her smile and gesture would be her key to survival. Many people would stare as she walked down the street; and when she heard all the yelling and whistling, she knew it was for her, so she'd secretly smile to herself while swaying her hips back and forth.

At the tender age of fourteen, Crystal Tradwell was still a virgin. She had only kissed a few boys while playing games at school, so she'd earned a reputation of being a tease.

Her first night of being homeless, Crystal was cold and didn't have a clue where her next meal would come from. While wandering around drowsily, she stumbled upon a small motel that had a lobby, so she'd entered the building with hopes of finding a sofa or somewhere warm to sleep. The air inside the motel was thick and smelled of mildew, but she hadn't let that bother her. She was more concerned with finding something good to eat and a comfortable place to lie down for the night. "Can I help you, miss?" a man asked in a raspy voice.

Crystal was startled. The voice seemed to be coming from behind the counter, but she hadn't seen anyone. The clerk finally made himself visible. He'd been sitting on a small stool behind the counter. He was a skinny white man who appeared to be somewhere around his mid to late twenties with a few missing teeth and long sideburns. "Are you lost, miss?"

"No," Crystal replied in a girl-like voice.

"What are you doing in here all by yourself so late at night?"

"I'm looking for something to eat and somewhere to sleep," she answered honestly.

"How old are you, and where are your parents?" the man asked while staring at her.

"I'm sixteen, and I don't have any parents."

The man knew she was lying because she looked nowhere near sixteen, but after looking her over and seeing how well developed she was, he decided he'd help her. "Do you have any money?" he asked nicely.

"No," Crystal whispered.

"Well, sweetheart, I can give you something to eat and a room to sleep in for tonight, but I can't do much more than that."

"That'll be cool," she said with a smile.

"My name is Joe. What's yours?"

"Crystal."

"Well, Crystal, that's a pretty name for a pretty girl."

"Thank you."

"Let's go find your room."

After grabbing the room key and locking the office door behind him, Joe led Crystal down a dimly lit hallway. They reached room number 20, which happened to be the last room at the very end of the hallway. Joe opened the room door and took Crystal on a tour of the small room. She thought the man was acting rather strange because he was pointing out obvious things to her, such as the twin-size bed, the small bathroom, and an old black-and-white television set, which he said was only there in case she got bored during the night. Joe told Crystal to make herself at home and that he'd be back with some food in only a few minutes. "You like hamburgers?" he asked.

"Yeah," Crystal answered.

Minutes later, Joe was entering the deli next door to the small motel. He grabbed a small bag of Doritos, two ready-made cheeseburgers, a few napkins, and a straw for the large fountain drink he'd made. After handing the clerk a five-dollar bill, he told the woman to keep the change as he exited the store.

Once back inside the motel, Joe's heart began to beat with anticipation. He took something from a small black duffel bag that was inside the office before heading back down the hallway toward Crystal's room. He knocked softly on the door before announcing his name, but Crystal had barely heard it. She was so tired that she'd fallen asleep on the small bed shortly after Joe had left. When she climbed from the bed and opened the door, Joe was glaring down at her while holding up the food he'd just bought for her. "Here, sweetheart, I got some food here for you," he said while handing her the brown paper bag. "Eat your food and sleep well. I'll see you in the morning," he said before walking away.

"Thank you," Crystal replied before closing the door. She turned on the television before climbing on the bed to eat her food. After drinking the ice-cold soda and chewing the last bite of her cheeseburger, Crystal was terribly tired, so she turned off the television and went to bed.

When she woke up the next morning, she didn't understand what had happened. Her body was in a tremendous amount of pain, and she slowly began to cry after noticing that her clothes had been ripped from her body. Dried blood was covering both sides of her inner thighs and was all over the bed where she'd slept.

Crystal was completely dumbfounded as to what had happened and had no memory at all of the night before. She climbed off the bed in an attempt to go to the bathroom, but fell to the floor when she tried to walk. Her ass was in pain, and she had no idea what to do. After placing a hand between her ass cheeks, she began to panic when she felt the warm blood streaming through her fingers and down her wrist. The sight of all the blood had been too much for Crystal to handle. She remembered being so horrified that she'd had to hold her breath while crawling to the bathroom.

* * *

Seven years later, Crystal still remembers how helpless she'd felt. She'd unwillingly lost her virginity to someone who'd brutally raped and sodomized her, and she still wasn't sure who did it or how it happened. She only knows that she had been alone when she'd gone to bed that night. Although she did have suspicions, Crystal was so embarrassed by what happened that she had never told anyone about it. She remembers wanting to leave the motel room so badly and just forgetting about the entire night. The problem was, she would never forget about it. That single night had only been the beginning of the seven years she'd have to endure of selling her body to survive. Crystal has been sexually involved with countless men and women since that terrible night, so not only does she now do it all, but she does it well.

At the young age of twenty-one, Crystal was in deep thought as the large jetliner left the ground. She'd heard many wonderful stories about Las Vegas, and she only hoped that it would be everything that everybody said it was. She'd saved some money, but now worried that what she'd managed to save would not be enough.

As the plane began its journey across the big blue skies, Crystal closed her eyes and began to think about her new life that lies ahead.

Chapter 3

When the plane landed at Las Vegas's McCarran Airport, Crystal was already looking for the exit. She'd taken a short nap during the flight; now she was anxious to find out what Las Vegas was all about.

After exiting the plane, she went to locate her luggage. She only had one medium-size suitcase and two carry-on bags, but it had still taken her a half an hour to find it. She was very new to this traveling thing, so she really didn't know what to do. It was her first time ever being outside of the state of Georgia, but after reading a few signs and asking for assistance, she had managed to find out exactly where she'd needed to go in order to find her luggage and catch a cab.

Once outside, Crystal asked a middle-aged cab driver if he'd assist her in finding a reasonably priced motel. She didn't have any money to waste, so she knew that she had to manage it well. The cab driver asked if she'd prefer a room downtown or on the Strip, but Crystal hadn't known the difference between the two, so she requested whichever one would be the cheapest.

After recommending Fremont Street, Crystal accepted, so the cab driver opened the door and allowed her to place her luggage inside the cab's backseat.

Once they'd left the airport's parking lot, Crystal found herself fascinated by the beautiful lights that lined the Las Vegas Strip. She'd tried seeing everything at once, but couldn't focus too long on anything because she was also keeping a close eye on the cab's meter. She'd managed to save six thousand dollars, but she knew that it wouldn't last too long. It was Friday night, so she'd decided that she'd have all weekend to tour as much of the city as possible before going to look for a job on Monday. The cab driver had suddenly interrupted her thoughts when he began to point out different buildings and sceneries while riding down Las Vegas Boulevard. He hadn't been driving fast at all, so Crystal became concerned because the meter had already reached eighteen dollars, and they still hadn't reached the downtown motel. "How much farther do we have to go?" she asked nervously.

"Oh, we'll be there in five minutes," he answered calmly. He'd noticed the nervousness in Crystal's voice when she'd spoke. He had been observing her through the cab's rearview mirror ever since they'd left the airport, so he was already aware of her watching the meter since entering the cab. "Don't worry about the meter, sweetheart. Just give me whatever you think is fair when we get to the motel," he said before turning off the meter.

"Thank you," Crystal replied while smiling.

The remainder of the trip was done in mere silence, but Crystal seemed much more relaxed. They'd finally reached the motel where she'd be staying, and she couldn't wait to get out of the cab. Her legs had severely cramped up, so she'd desperately wanted to stretch them out. After walking around in a few small circles, Crystal removed twenty-five dollars from her purse and handed it to the cab driver. He smiled as he accepted the money before stuffing it inside the front pocket of his baggy jeans. "Need help?" he asked nicely.

"Yes, please," Crystal answered.

After accepting the cab driver's help, she grabbed the two carry-on bags while allowing him to grab the heavier suitcase.

"Thank you," she said.

"No problem."

The cab driver followed closely behind as Crystal walked toward the motel's front office. He was really appreciating the view. He'd already known that Crystal was beautiful, but he hadn't known that she possessed what he considered to be the perfect body. Not only did she have a perfectly round ass, but she also had a set of hips and thighs that were guaranteed to grab any man's attention. As they entered the motel's front office, it seemed that every light inside the building had been turned on. It was extremely bright, and the air inside seemed tremendously cold as they approached the counter.

After sitting the luggage in front of the counter, Crystal thanked the cab driver again as he wished her well in Las Vegas. He'd already known in his mind that she would be fine, so he backed toward the same door that they'd just entered while leaving her at the counter.

Once Crystal had settled into her room, she turned on the television. It was eleven o'clock at night, so she slowly flipped through the channels before deciding on watching the news. The news anchors were an immediate reminder that she was no longer in Atlanta, and she found herself intrigued by the city of Las Vegas in the background. It was still kind of early, so she decided on taking a peek at the Las Vegas nightlife. She took a quick shower and changed her clothes before stuffing a twenty-dollar bill in the back pocket of her tight-fitting Levis. After leaving the room, Crystal began her stroll up Fremont Street. She was careful to observe everything around the area to be sure that she'd be able to find her way back to her room. With every step she took, Crystal gained more confidence and believed that her life in Las Vegas would be just fine. She looked around before noticing that several people had been staring in her direction. *You still got it, girl. This may be a new city, but turning heads is nothing new for you,* she thought to herself. She'd suddenly began to feel at ease, so she walked casually inside a nearby 7-Eleven and purchased a cherry slurpee. She wished that she'd pocketed a smaller bill, but she handed the twenty-dollar bill to the convenience store clerk and waited for her change.

After leaving the store, Crystal sipped the slurpee through a long red straw while continuing her stroll up Fremont Street. While being observant, she noticed several women who appeared to be prostitutes, along with a few men who looked like pimps. A lot of others appeared to be tourists, but all Crystal could think about at the moment was the life she'd left in Atlanta, Georgia.

After thinking and quickening her pace, everything was suddenly wiped from her mind when she found herself mesmerized by the beautiful array of lights that shined above her. Crystal smiled and looked around before an older women tapped her on the shoulder, "It's called the Fremont Street experience."

Crystal smiled at the older women before replying, "It's beautiful. I'm new in town, and I've never seen anything like this before."

The older woman smiled at Crystal before ducking into a nearby gift shop. She'd seen many people who'd been infatuated by the lights of Las Vegas, so she moved on without giving it a second thought. Crystal had not been the first, nor would she be the last who'd enjoy viewing the colorful lights of the Fremont Street experience.

Crystal stood there watching the lights for another fifteen minutes before deciding that it was probably time for her to head back toward the motel. She had a few loose coins in her pocket after buying the slurpee, so she stopped just beyond the doorway of a casino and tried her luck at the slot machines.

It was now after midnight, but since the downtown streets were still crowded with people, Crystal decided against rushing back to the motel. She figured having a good time was what Vegas was all about, so she played the slot machines and drank free cocktails until two o'clock in the morning. She'd become somewhat intoxicated and had lost nineteen dollars, so she knew that it was time for her to go back to her motel room before calling it a night. She hurried back toward her room, paying little attention to anything other than the traffic and strangers, which happened to be everybody because she didn't know anybody.

Crystal returned to the motel and smiled to herself as she read a sign on a billboard across the street. It read the Lucky Lady Motel, and although she wasn't feeling too lucky herself after losing nineteen dollars, she was feeling extremely good about herself and the decision she'd made to move to Las Vegas to start a new life. After entering her room and closing the door behind her, Crystal felt the same sensation that the cab driver had felt earlier. She breathed a sigh of relief and laughed out loud because she knew that she would be all right.

Chapter 4

Early Monday morning, Billy Brocks was in deep thought as he neared the Clark County Courthouse. He sipped the black coffee that he'd just purchased from Starbucks, but he was also upset because his new secretary, Yvonne, had failed to file a motion for a continuance that he'd need in order to help one of his clients. Simone would have taken care of it, but she had an important appointment with her gynecologist that Friday, so the new secretary had been expected to take care of it.

Billy's case involved a witness that couldn't be located, so he was hoping that the judge would grant him the extra time that he'd need in order to locate his female witness. He figured that he could explain the situation to the court, and after hearing his explanation, the judge would be obliged to grant his oral request.

When Billy arrived inside the courtroom, he didn't have to wait long because the judge called his case first. After the case was called, Billy stood up and nicely explained to the court that a motion for a continuance had been prepared, but since he'd recently hired a new secretary, she had failed to file the motion on Friday. That's the reason it wasn't inside the case file to be considered by the court. "Objection, Your Honor!" the district attorney blurted out. "This case has been pending inside this courtroom for six months now, and the state is prepared to prosecute. Mr. Brocks's request should be denied so we can get this case out of the way and move on to other things."

"Your Honor, with all due respect, I just finished pouring my heart out to this court, explaining that I have a female witness who could prove that my client is innocent, but she's missing and it would be impossible for me to proceed and properly represent my client or his best interest without first locating my witness," Billy pleaded.

"Your Honor, this man does not care about the best interest of his client, nor does he show any respect for this court. He's been living and surviving off the reputation of his father and grandfather, and he thinks that he'll be able to ride their coattails forever!" the district attorney said angrily.

Billy was completely shocked by the district attorney's statement, and he could feel his anger boiling inside of him. "Your Honor, this is very uncalled for from the district attorney. I don't understand where all of this animosity is coming from, but I do understand that he's way out of line for bringing my late father and grandfather into this."

The judge, along with many others inside the crowded courtroom was stunned by the exchange of words that they'd just witnessed between Billy Brocks and the district attorney. Judge Oram was at a lost for words, so Prosecutor Philip Doolittle continued, "The mob doesn't run Las Vegas anymore, so Mr. Brocks cannot expect for things to go his way every time he makes a request to this court, unless he's paid the judge off or some other government official like his father and grandfather used to do!" He ended boldly.

Billy became so enraged by the comment that he'd run over and began punching the older man repeatedly in the face until the bailiff and other defense attorneys had come over and pulled him off. Billy hadn't realized what he'd done until after it was over with. "Order in this court!" The judge yelled while slamming his gavel repeatedly on top of a wooden block. "ORDER IN THE COURT!" he repeated.

The entire courtroom had gone into pandemonium as they watched what was taking place. They'd been scrambling around and couldn't believe what they'd just witnessed. No one could have ever guessed that this kind of episode would have taken place in a court of law. The district attorney's face was a bloody mess and had quickly swelled while everybody was scrambling around trying to help him up from the courtroom floor. The bailiff asked that someone call 911 so the district attorney could receive the medical attention that he desperately needed. The courtroom was immediately cleared except for the judge, the bailiff, and the young Billy Brocks who was very uncomfortable after being sat down on a chair with a set of cold, hard handcuffs clamped tightly on his wrists. Judge Oram was staring directly at Billy as he scolded him in the presence of the bailiff. He reminded him that he had taken an oath to practice law in a professional manner, but that oath had just been violated. He also made comments despising Billy for his unethical conduct and spoke very harshly before charging him with contempt of court. The judge stated that he'd personally felt that Billy should be disbarred for such behavior, but it would be up to the Las Vegas Bar Association to make that decision. Judge Oram instructed the bailiff to place Billy inside a holding cell by himself, and he wasn't to be let out until he authorized it. The judge added that he wanted Billy to think long and hard about what he'd done while he'd be deciding what he would do about punishment.

Thinking long and hard was exactly what Billy Brocks had been doing. He still couldn't believe what he'd done. He'd chosen a profession to help other people out of trouble, but now he found himself in jail with no one who could let him out except for the man who'd just put him there. Billy had all sorts of questions going through his mind. He'd never been out of control like that before and had been surprised by his own actions. Billy had never even had a real fistfight before, so he cracked a smile as he realized that he'd actually won one.

At four o'clock that evening, Billy was finally released from his holding cell. The bailiff apologized for keeping him in so long but explained that Judge Oram had just given him authorization. He'd calmed down tremendously after spending six hours inside the lonely, cold holding cell, but he tried showing compassion after the bailiff finished explaining that the district attorney had suffered a broken nose and a fractured jaw. Billy was in awe as he listened to the condition of Philip Doolittle, but his heart suddenly sank when the bailiff informed him that the man had promised to press charges. Billy stopped immediately in his tracks, and he couldn't believe it. At thirty-four years of age and one of the most prominent defense attorneys in Las Vegas, he didn't know what the future held for him. His conduct had violated every rule that the Bar Association stood for, and he wasn't sure if he'd still be permitted to practice law with criminal charges pending against him. It had simply become too much drama for one day, and Billy felt that he needed more time to sit back and sort through it all. He quickly got inside his BMW and called Brocks & Brocks Law Offices from his car phone. He tried explaining to his secretary, Simone, what had happened, but she stopped him as soon as he'd begun and said that she already knew about it. Billy wasn't aware that the entire incident had been publicized on the afternoon news a few hours after it had taken place. Every lawyer in town had been talking about it because most have been jealous of Billy Brocks ever since he'd begun practicing law. Most felt like they had to work twice as hard to make a name for themselves, but Billy Brocks had been introduced to the practice with a silver spoon in his mouth since his father and grandfather were both well-known attorneys themselves. Billy's name alone had been opening doors for him, and he usually got all the best clients over all the other well-known attorneys. They felt that Billy's name had been working for him even when he did no work himself. Billy realized that a lot of people hated him just because he's the son and grandson of the father-son duo,

Edwin Brocks, Sr., and Edwin Brocks, Jr. He now understood where the district attorney's animosity had come from, so he placed the blame on his family's name for his current predicament.

After all, it was the two men's past that everyone really hated. Billy had no clue what their past was, but he knew that whatever it was, it had come back to haunt him. Both men had long been dead, so everyone had been taking their frustrations out on Billy. The young attorney with an impeccable reputation was now in trouble with the law himself, and he worried because his future as a licensed attorney was now in jeopardy.

Chapter 5

Crystal had become frustrated with her job search. After being in Las Vegas for thirty days, she was still living in the cheap motel downtown. Her six thousand dollars savings had been cut in half, so she was becoming desperate for a job.

While sitting Indian-style in the middle of her room floor, Crystal searched carefully through the classified section of the Sunday newspaper. She wasn't looking for anything specific because she needed to find whatever job she could in order to earn an income.

So far, she had only been spending money and not earning any, so she knew that cycle had to be reversed. A few minutes after searching the paper, an advertisement caught Crystal's eye. It simply read Girls Needed before explaining that the girls could earn two to four thousand dollars per week, but it still hadn't explained what the girls would be doing.

In a small paragraph at the end of the advertisement, it stated that no experience would be necessary, and they would train the girls who had no experience. Crystal wondered what the girls would be doing, but didn't think too much about it because she had already decided that she needed the money and was willing to try whatever was necessary in order to get it. After carefully tearing the section from the newspaper, she made plans to be at the address early the following morning. Once she'd made the decision, she felt a little better about her situation, although it hadn't changed yet. She stood from the floor, picked up the newspaper, and neatly folded it before tossing it on top of her suitcase. She then began to make her bed while wondering what she'd do for the day.

It was a bright Sunday morning, and although the weather was nice, there wasn't too much that she wanted to do. She had already been to several of the casinos downtown and a few on the Strip, so she didn't want to do any of that. Crystal's focus was on making some money because she really wanted to move from the cheap motel and into a more permanent residence. She also needed to buy a car because she had become tired of catching the bus and wasting money on cab fare. She'd already decided that catching cabs was out of the question because not only were they too expensive, but the cab drivers had still expected a tip once the trip was over. It had become too much for Crystal and it made her realize how kindhearted the cab driver had been who'd driven her downtown from the airport when she arrived in Las Vegas. No driver since then had been as nice as him. While contemplating about what she'd do that day, Crystal opened her suitcase to look for something clean to wear. She badly needed to do laundry because most of her clothes were dirty. While searching the luggage for something to wear, she'd ended up making two piles of dirty laundry in the middle of the floor. All the colored clothes were in one pile while all the whites were in another. She had learned a couple of weeks earlier while taking a walk around the area that the motel had a small washroom. She decided on having breakfast at a soul food restaurant that was located across the street from the motel and made a mental note to get a few dollars in quarters while she was there.

After taking a hot shower, Crystal brushed her teeth and stood naked in front of the bathroom mirror while admiring her curvaceous figure. After all she'd been through in her twenty-one years of life, it was hard to believe that a body so perfect had been used and abused the way hers had. She reminisced about some of the frightening times that she'd experienced in Atlanta. While carefully looking over her figure, her eyes began to water as she remembered the times when some of her tricks had gotten out of hand with some of their bizarre sex acts. She quickly wiped her eyes and pushed the thoughts from her mind, because erasing the awful past was her main reason for coming to Las Vegas. She'd already made plans to do laundry later on that morning; so after putting on lotion and spraying perfume, Crystal slipped into a pair of tight-fitting, faded blue jeans and no panties underneath along with a pullover sweatshirt and no bra. She placed a ten-dollar bill in her back pocket, brushed her long curly hair, and hurried out of the motel's front door. While waiting at the crosswalk, her stomach began to growl as her eyes became fixated on the restaurant across the street. Once inside the soul food restaurant, the strong aroma of fried bacon quickly filled Crystal's nostrils as she picked up a menu and seated herself at a small table near the restaurant's emergency exit. She glanced at her room while looking across the street from the restaurant's side window. A maid had just finished cleaning the room next door to hers and was about to leave in the opposite direction. Crystal had already made it clear to the motel's manager that the maids were not to clean her room unless she requested it. She didn't want or trust anyone inside of her room while she wasn't there. "Hi, may I take your order?" a tall black waitress asked.

"Yes, I'll have some eggs, bacon, and a few slices of toast," Crystal answered quickly.

"Would you like your eggs prepared a certain way?"

"Scrambled, please."

"And would you like anything to drink with that?"

"I'll have some orange juice."

"I'll be right back with that."

Crystal smiled to herself as the waitress walked away. The tall, pretty woman had always been nice to her when she'd come to the restaurant, so Crystal had always tried to sit at the same table every time in hopes of having the woman as her waitress. She had never said much to the woman besides hello, but Crystal had always left a two-dollar tip because the woman's attitude had always been so nice. When the waitress returned, she smiled as she sat a tall glass of orange juice and a glass of ice water in front of Crystal. "Your food will be here shortly," she said without looking at Crystal.

"Thank you," Crystal replied softly.

After finishing her breakfast, Crystal felt a lot better. She sat at her table and watched the traffic for a while before going up to the cashier to pay for her food. She'd almost forgot to get the few dollars in quarters that she needed in order to do her laundry, but was suddenly reminded when the cashier opened the cash drawer.

After getting three dollars in quarters, Crystal took her time about walking across the street toward her room.

Inside the room, she left the door partially open because she had no intentions of staying long. She stuffed the two loads of clothes inside a laundry basket that she'd bought at a thrift store a few weeks earlier. She carefully placed a brown paper bag containing bleach, and laundry detergent on top of the basket before leaving the room.

Later that evening, she laid a hot pink Nike sweat suit across the bed that she planned to wear to the address that she'd gotten out of the newspaper earlier that day. She wanted to get some sleep so that she'd be able to wake up early enough to make it there on time.

After watching television for a while, she found herself sleepy, so she turned off the television before crawling under the warm covers. She drifted off to sleep as she lay there, wondering what the next day held for her.

Chapter 6

It has been over a month since Billy's courtroom incident, and he still didn't know what the Bar Association was going to do about sanctioning him, but he just hoped it would all be over soon. He did receive a fax and a personal visit from a bar representative a couple of days after the incident. He was informed that he was no longer permitted inside any courtroom unless he was scheduled to make an appearance in the criminal case that was now pending against him.

Billy had been forced to return money to several of his clients because he wouldn't be allowed to represent them inside the courtroom, and that's what he'd been hired to do. However, the Bar Association did allow him to continue doing work that consisted only of paperwork. He could still file appeals, motions, post-conviction petitions, and things of that sort on behalf of his clients.

The Bar Association had also informed him that they would be waiting until his criminal case was resolved before launching an investigation of their own against him.

Billy was trying his best to pretend that he hadn't been affected by all the drama, but Simone and a lot of other employees of Brocks & Brocks had clearly saw the change in him. The new secretary, Yvonne, had been terminated the day after his courtroom incident. Billy thought it had all been her fault in the first place, because if she had done her job and filed the motion the minute he had handed it to her, he would have never had to ask the judge for a continuance, he thought. Simone was now his only secretary, and he has been overworking her with tons of paperwork that he asked to have typed and filed on a daily basis. Simone was fully aware that he was going through a hard time and trying to cope with his legal problems, but she didn't think it was a good enough excuse for him to mistreat her, especially when she'd been nothing but nice to him.

Billy didn't want to waste any money by hiring another secretary to take Yvonne's place, so he decided to give Simone a reasonable raise. The pending assault charge was beginning to take its toll on Billy Brocks. He had become overwhelmed by all the pressure he'd received on a daily basis, and he wanted it all to stop. He called on Michael Shoemaker to represent him. Mr. Shoemaker was a well-known attorney in California's Bay Area that his late father had used a couple of times when he was in trouble. The hotshot attorney resides in San Francisco but is also licensed to practice law in Nevada. By Billy being an attorney himself, no other attorney in Las Vegas could legally represent him without there being a conflict of interest.

Billy's appearance was gradually changing for the worse. He hadn't been taking pride in his style of dress the way he'd been known for in the past. He no longer shaved on a daily basis, and Simone had often smelled alcohol on his breath when he showed up at the office, but that's something she kept to herself. She just wanted to continue doing her job the same way she always had, but Billy had begun to interfere with that as well. He constantly broke appointments with his clients and left it up to Simone to come up with different excuses to tell them.

Brocks & Brocks Law Offices was not operating as smoothly as it once had and neither was Billy Brocks.

Chapter 7

Crystal exited the bus on the Las Vegas Strip just a few minutes too early. She'd been searching for the address that was given in the newspaper advertisement, but ended up having to walk two blocks before she found it. As she approached the brightly colored building, she stared at the large sign that stood in front of it. The sign read Lickety Splits, so she paused for a few moments before going inside. As she entered the building, the thought crossed her mind that maybe she was late because there was already several other girls who were waiting inside. The girls were of different nationalities, and Crystal found herself amazed at how beautiful they all were. They were all waiting inside a small lobby because they had been instructed to hold tight by an older woman who was standing only a few feet away holding a clipboard. The woman approached Crystal soon after she'd entered the building and nicely introduced herself. "Hi, I'm Stacy. Are you here to apply for a job?"

"Yes, am I late?" Crystal asked.

"No, you're just in time, but I need you to fill out some basic information before I can even consider you as an applicant."

Crystal grabbed the clipboard as it was being handed to her and provided her name, age, height, weight, measurements, and her nationality before handing the clipboard back to the woman.

An hour later, a man entered through a side door carrying the same clipboard that the woman had been carrying earlier. He called for the girls' attention and asked that they quiet down to hear what he had to say. "All right, girls, I want to thank all of you for coming out, but I'll only be hiring ten of you," he said before continuing. "I'll be keeping twenty of you here, then I'll pick the best ten of the twenty girls. I've already studied the information you've all provided, and since I'll be needing a variety of everything, I picked the girls that mostly fit the mixture that I'm looking for. When I call your name, I need you to step over here to the right please. If I don't call your name, I do appreciate you for coming out, but I won't be needing you, so I ask that you leave the building," he said bluntly.

All of the girls grew tense. They were all hoping that their names would be called because they did not want to be embarrassed by having to leave. After eighteen of their names had been called, Crystal began to worry. The man carefully studied his list before announcing the next name. "Crystal Tradwell."

Crystal quietly walked over to where the other eighteen girls were standing. She wanted to smile, but somehow managed to suppress it. Soon after, only twenty girls remained. All the others had been sent home. The remaining girls were all instructed to line up in tandem order by the large man while he stood back and gave each one a once-over before pointing them out and asking them to leave. Crystal stood nervously while wishing that she'd worn something other than the hot pink Nike sweat suit. It could easily be seen that she had a nice body, but she didn't feel confident that the sweat suit was revealing all that she had to offer.

The man had already called nine of the girls to leave, and Crystal was relieved when he didn't call her as the tenth. "Congratulations!" the man said while staring at the remaining ten girls. "You're the ten finalists that I've chosen to hire as entertainers here at Lickety Splits. I'm your boss, Barry Licks, as well as the club's owner." Barry paused and looked around before continuing, "I need all of you to fill out applications and sign contracts inside the door to your left," he said while pointing. "We pay you in cash here at Lickety Splits, and if you already know how to dance, some of you will be starting tonight. If you don't know how to dance, we'll be training you in sessions at noon tomorrow. The option is yours whether you want to go topless or all the way, whichever you feel most comfortable with, but I suggest that you read all the rules and regulations of the club before starting your shift because there are some strict consequences for any violations. So please take the time to read the handbook. You'll all be instructed on exactly what to do after you fill out the applications and sign the contracts. Good luck to all of you, and I wish you well as entertainers at Lickety Splits. I'll be seeing some of you tonight."

Crystal was in deep thought while riding the bus back downtown. She'd filled out her application and signed the basic contract after it was explained to her. She'd been scheduled to report to work at eight o'clock that night since she already knew how to dance. It wasn't exactly the lifestyle she'd planned to lead when she came to Las Vegas; but dancing would establish an income, which she desperately needed, so she wasn't too hard on herself. She entered her room at the downtown motel and dived on the bed. She knew that her nights of sleeping in the small bed were numbered, and she was anxious as she closed her eyes to wonder what her future would be like.

Chapter 8

At twelve thirty Tuesday morning, Billy Brocks was cruising the Las Vegas Strip in his brand-new SUV. He'd taken a nap earlier in the day, so he wasn't feeling tired at all. He would have to be at work later on that morning, but since he didn't have a certain time to be at the office, he really wasn't concerned about how late he stayed out at night. All Billy wanted to do now was have a few drinks and forget about everything that was taking place in his life.

After passing up all the casinos, he pulled his Yukon into a semicrowded parking lot. It was still a weekday, so a lot of people weren't out and about at that time of morning. He activated the alarm by using the remote control located on his keychain as soon as he'd gotten out of the large SUV. He glanced down at his clothes to make sure he was presentable before entering the barely lit building.

Billy was allowed free admission, but was informed at the door that there was a two-drink minimum if he chose to stay. He'd definitely wanted a drink, so he had no problem with buying at least two.

Once inside, Billy had another set of twin doors to walk through before he clearly heard the loud music. He watched a sexy young blonde as she danced seductively on stage. She danced to an up-tempo pop song, and Billy continued to watch closely while walking toward the stage to find a seat. He didn't make it a habit to frequent many places such as Lickety Splits, but with all the drama that was taking place in his life, he thought he'd needed a change.

As soon as he'd found a seat and sat down, a short but well-endowed brunette approached him to take his order. He ordered a beer and a seven and seven while sitting directly in front of the stage and watching as the blonde girl ended her routine by sliding up and down a brass pole.

The music began to blare right after the blonde had left the stage, so Billy waited for the next performance. He almost stood from his chair when the next girl entered the stage from behind a curtain. She was beautiful, and the music she'd chosen was an R&B type. The girl danced slowly and more provocatively as the song got underway. Billy was amazed by the young woman's beauty, and although he'd never dated or even considered dating a woman outside of his culture, he was terribly attracted to this young woman.

He couldn't figure out what her nationality was, but the fact that she wasn't white hadn't meant anything to Billy Brocks. He tried his best to ignore the young woman's beauty, but couldn't resist as she swirled her curvaceous body. Her long black hair, perfectly round ass, and slightly slanted eyes were all perfect with her golden skin complexion that glowed under the dim stage light.

Billy was so focused on all her curves that he hadn't even noticed that the young woman had been staring back at him. He watched with his mouth partially open as she swayed her hips back and forth. When he finally glanced up and caught her eyes, she quickly averted them to another direction. Her set was finally over, so the young woman quickly left the stage without another glance.

Billy watched carefully, hoping the young woman would turn around and look again, but she never did. After she'd left the stage, Billy stood in frustration before leaving the club with plans of going home and going to bed.

It was now 1:55 a.m., Billy hadn't known it, but the club would be closing in five minutes. He drove down the empty stretch of highway, going over the speed limit as he thought about the woman he'd just seen in the strip club.

Little did he know but the beautiful young woman was inside a cab, traveling in the opposite direction on her way home, thinking about him.

Chapter 9

Later that morning, Billy showed up at the office at eleven o'clock. Simone had an attitude because she had become tired of Billy acting like he didn't care about what was going on in his life. She was also tired of lying and making up excuses for Billy's clients about why he wasn't in the office or why he hadn't been returning their phone calls to inform them of their current case status. "What's wrong with you, Billy?" Simone yelled.

"Everything is wrong, Simone!"

"Billy, I know that this is a hard time for you, but you have to pull yourself together and prove that you're still capable of being a good lawyer," she said in a softer voice.

"Lawyers practice law inside the courtroom, Simone, so how am I supposed to prove anything to anybody?"

Simone realized that it hadn't been a good time to talk to her boss, so she angrily slammed the door to Billy's office before returning to her desk.

Billy sat at his desk in frustration before flipping open his laptop to check his e-mail, but he didn't have any. He then checked to see if a court date had been set in his assault case, but no date had been set yet. He'd been wanting to apologize to the district attorney he'd assaulted, but the bar representative who had paid him a visit had personally advised him against it. They warned him that he could be arrested and thrown in jail until trial if they found out he'd tried to make contact with the victim in his case. Billy hadn't known it, but the district attorney had also been forbidden against contacting him.

With both Simone and Billy sitting angrily at their desks, that section of Brocks & Brocks appeared to be anything but an attorney's office. There were no phones ringing, no fax machines operating, no paperwork being prepared, or no one talking. Simone sat at her desk and admired her freshly done manicure while Billy sat fully reclined at his desk, looking up at the ceiling, and fantasizing about the exotic-looking dancer that he'd seen at Lickety Splits just hours earlier.

Chapter 10

Around noon the following day, Crystal was awakened by what sounded like someone pounding on the motel's front door. When she rose to a sitting position, she realized that the sound was coming from the room next door to hers. She had been hearing the sound several times a day ever since the young couple had moved in a few days earlier. She figured that it could only be the headboard hitting the wall because she could still hear the woman screaming and moaning from whatever pleasure the man was giving her. She lay back on the bed and listened intensely as the couple continued to make love.

Crystal had been sleeping at least until noon every day since she'd started working at the club. Although she'd only been working there for a couple of nights, she was happy about the tips she'd made so far. Her first night of dancing, she had only gone topless, but other girls had quickly told her that going all the way was where the money was. The second night, she'd tried it and was very surprised to learn that the other girls had been right. She hadn't really talked to many of the other girls, but she had met one by the name of Angel who had been looking out for her and showing her the ropes since she'd been at the club. Angel was the girlfriend of one of the bouncers who works at the club. She's a light-skinned black girl with the kind of body that even Crystal admired. Angel has been a dancer at Lickety Splits for six months, and her dreams were to someday save enough money to open up her own strip club.

Crystal lay in bed naked. She'd been so tired after coming home from work that she'd found it a lot easier and a lot quicker to just get in bed right after taking a shower. She had a ton of things on her mind, but after listening to the couple make love next door, she realized that she hadn't been with anyone since leaving Atlanta. Her nipples had swollen up, so she gently rolled them between her fingers before allowing her hand to ease toward the wet spot between her legs. She wished that she'd had a vibrator, but since she hadn't thought to buy one, her fingers would have to do the trick for now. Crystal opened her legs as wide as she could and began rubbing firmly on her clit until reaching orgasm. Content for the moment, she got out of bed and headed for the bathroom to take a shower. She had a few things planned throughout the week, and moving out of the small motel was one of them. She'd no longer had to worry about calling a cab or catching the bus to or from work because Angel owned a car and had promised to pick her up and drop her back off every day they worked together. That happened to be every day because the girls made out their own schedules at Lickety Splits.

Angel recommended that Crystal move somewhere on the Las Vegas Strip because it was closer to the job and would be less of a hassle for both of them to get to and from work. She recommended a place called the Budget Suites and said that they were much nicer than the small motel downtown. She said that Crystal would only be a block away from the job and within walking distance to everything that she'd need until buying her own car.

Crystal agreed to move to the Budget Suites on the coming weekend, and Angel agreed to help even though there were only a few things to move.

Crystal was expecting Angel to be at the motel to pick her up at three o'clock. They had made plans to go to the mall to pick up a few items. Crystal wanted to buy a few sets of thong panties and matching bras that she thought would look good as part of her act at Lickety Splits. She had no idea what Angel wanted to buy, but it was already two o'clock, and she had to get dressed before Angel arrived.

Chapter 11

Billy Brocks was finally going to get his day in court. He hadn't even known that a court date had been set until his late father's attorney, Michael Shoemaker, had flown in from San Francisco the day before. The two men met in Billy's office to discuss the strategy they'd use to get Billy the best deal possible. Neither man thought he'd have a chance of being acquitted if he decided on going to trial.

Simone had taken it upon herself and decided that Billy should learn a lesson, so she chose not to tell him about the court date that she'd known about for a couple of days. She and Billy hadn't said much to each other in the past few days, and when they did, the conversation usually escalated into an argument.

After discussing the evidence that the state had against Billy, Michael Shoemaker thought that it would be in his best interest to plead guilty to a lesser offense. If Billy tried to plead not guilty, the prosecutor would have a field day putting him on trial, and that's what they'd planned to prevent.

Billy wanted to resolve the case as soon as possible without having his license revoked to practice law. The victim Philip Doolittle was a well-known district attorney who had several other credible witnesses that would corroborate his story.

By Billy being a criminal attorney himself, he didn't need the advice of Michael Shoemaker to know that pleading guilty to the lesser offense would be in his best interest. They assumed that he would only get probation and possibly a fine, but still be able to keep his license to practice law.

Resolving the criminal case would not be the end of Billy's legal troubles, he still had the Bar Association to deal with and their decision would probably be based on the outcome of his criminal case.

At eight thirty the following morning, Billy casually strolled inside the Clark County Courthouse with his attorney Michael Shoemaker by his side. He hadn't been inside the building since the courtroom incident, and he could feel that everybody was staring at him. He walked quickly passed several attorneys, prosecutors, and court clerks that he'd known for many years, but some didn't even acknowledge his presence.

Billy had proudly strolled inside the courtroom numerous times before, but this time was different. He'd hoped that it would all be over soon because the man they'd described as being bold and brazen was now embarrassed and scared. Billy had come to this building on many occasions to help other men and women get out of trouble, but now he was the one who needed somebody to help him. He had been offered a plea bargain, but it hadn't been the one he or his attorney was hoping for. The prosecutor was asking that he explain why he'd acted in such an unethical manner, and that he beg for the court's mercy. They wanted Billy to plead guilty to assault, do six months on probation, and pay a fine to the victim Philip Doolittle for his lost wages and pain and suffering.

After Billy stood in front of the court and pled guilty, he tried to explain what happened, but Judge Oram, who Billy had known and considered a friend for many years, quickly cut him off. "We don't need to hear your mouth anymore, Mr. Brocks. You've already done enough damage to yourself, and you don't need to make it worse," the judge said coldly.

Billy was very offended by the judge's remark, but he somehow managed to hold himself together. A sentencing date was set to be held in thirty days, and it was Judge Oram this time who'd told Billy that he still wasn't allowed inside the courtroom until sentencing.

Billy walked briskly out of the courtroom with his attorney at his side. They hadn't said a word to each other until it was time for them to part ways outside the courtroom. They had no reason to see each other again until sentencing, so Michael Shoemaker headed in the direction of the airport to fly back to San Francisco while Billy Brocks had no clue where he was headed.

Billy ended up back at his office, but not before stopping at the liquor store. He thought that things would be a lot better once he'd gone to court, but he was wrong. He'd been born and raised to be an attorney, and he didn't know how to be anything else. He paced the length of his office for half an hour while trying to figure out what to do. The problem was he didn't know what to do, so he removed one of the two shot bottles of gin from his inside jacket pocket before drinking it all in a single gulp. That bottle was immediately followed by the second bottle, and after pacing for a while longer, he called Simone into his office. She immediately smelled the strong scent of alcohol as soon as she'd entered, but Billy hadn't tried hiding it because he was still standing there with the shot bottle in his hand when she walked in. "Simone, I wanna say that I'm sorry for the way that I've been acting lately. I know I've been acting like an asshole, but I'm scared of where my life is headed," he said as tears welled in his eyes.

Simone didn't say a word. She had never seen Billy's sensitive side before, so she stared at him before walking up and wrapping her arms around him. It seemed that affection was all Billy had needed because he no longer held back his tears. He held Simone's body tightly in his arms for several minutes before letting her go. Being the sweetheart that she is, Simone consoled her boss before recommending that he go home for the weekend.

It was Friday, so Billy took Simone's advice and took the rest of the weekend off.

Chapter 12

Crystal was really enjoying the company of her new friend, Angel. The two had been spending a lot of time together and were beginning to learn a lot more about each other. They had become very comfortable around each other, giving each other compliments, and revealing some of their innermost secrets.

Angel's boyfriend, Frank, had begun not to like when the two girls get together; although he adored Crystal, he had become jealous of her because it seemed that Angel was no longer giving him the quality time that she once had. The two girls had been seeing each other at work every night, but to them that still wasn't enough time.

Angel and Crystal had both been the only child growing up, and they'd both come from dysfunctional backgrounds and foster homes. The two girls had grown close, and it seemed that they had become inseparable.

On Friday evening, Crystal was extremely excited. She'd just finished moving into the Budget Suites, and Angel was right there by her side. Crystal smiled while giving Angel a warm hug and thanking her for all she had done. She was very content with her new life, and being content was something she hadn't remembered being in a long time. "I'll see you tonight, girl," Angel said while picking up her purse and preparing to leave.

"Where you goin'?" Crystal asked in a surprised voice.

"I gotta go home. Frank call himself mad at me because I've been spending all my time with you and not having time to give him some pussy," Angel said while laughing.

"All right, girl, I'll see you tonight, but don't let Frank tap that ass too hard and make you forget about coming back to pick me up."

"Girl, I like it hard sometimes," Angel replied before closing the door behind her.

Although neither girl could see each other, they both were still smiling at Angel's last remark.

Once Angel was gone, Crystal stretched her arms while looking around. She really like her new place and was proud of herself for making the kind of progress that she could finally see. She no longer had to go out to eat every time she got hungry because she now had a kitchenette that she and Angel had stocked with food. She also had a six-pack of beer that she'd placed in the refrigerator just in case she felt like getting tipsy.

Crystal made herself a warm bubble bath and closed her eyes while listening to the sultry sounds that came from her radio. It was the same radio station that Angel always listened to in her pearl white Nissan Maxima.

When her bubble bath was complete, Crystal dried her long black hair with a large bath towel while walking around her room. She'd felt so refreshed after taking the warm bath that she didn't even bother putting on any clothes. She took the time to lotion every inch of her smooth, soft skin before slipping into a pink silk bathrobe that she'd bought from the mall earlier that week. She didn't have to be at work for a few more hours, so she decided on drinking one of the ice-cold beers before relaxing on the sofa to rest her eyes. She'd already laid the outfit across the bed that she'd planned on wearing to work that night, so it wouldn't take her long to get dressed once Angel returned to pick her up. She lay on the sofa and listened to one of Vegas's most soulful radio stations before drifting off to sleep.

An hour later, Crystal's room door slowly crept open before a woman quietly entered. Crystal was not aware that she had company, so she continued to sleep comfortably on the couch.

As the woman slowly approached, she paused for a few seconds while staring at Crystal's beautiful face. She stared at Crystal's body before noticing that she wasn't wearing anything under the pink silk robe she was wearing. She focused on Crystal's thick, creamy thighs before running her hot, wet tongue across Crystal's stomach. As her tongue advanced toward Crystal's breasts, Crystal suddenly opened her eyes and was surprised to see that her best friend Angel was licking and sucking all over her swollen nipple.

By that time, Angel had fully opened Crystal's bathrobe and was sucking each breast back and forth. Crystal had become so wet between her legs that she eagerly wanted to feel Angel's tongue between them. Angel stared at Crystal with passion-filled eyes before leaning forward to kiss her deeply in the mouth. The two girls kissed passionately while Crystal moaned softly as Angel pushed two fingers inside of her. Crystal opened her legs and allowed Angel's fingers to prod deeper inside her slippery hole. Crystal moaned louder as Angel continued to kiss her neck while penetrating her love hole with expertise. This was Crystal's first sexual encounter since coming to Las Vegas, and she was really enjoying every minute of it.

Suddenly, Crystal's body began to shake. She opened her legs even wider before thrusting her hips forward to meet Angel's fingers. Crystal began screaming as her body continued to shake uncontrollably. She wrapped her arm around Angel's back and held her tightly as she reached orgasm. "Damn!" Crystal said in exhaustion.

"I've been wanting to do that for a while," Angel replied softly.

"I never expected you to do that."

"I figured since Frank just hooked me up, I'd come over to hook you up."

"You did a damn good job," Crystal said while climbing from the couch.

Crystal headed toward the bathroom to take another shower, but she'd purposely left her bathrobe on the couch to be sure that Angel would get a good look at her smooth round ass while she walked away. Angel knew immediately that she wanted some more of Crystal, but since they both had to be at work soon, she knew that it would have to wait until another time.

In the meantime, Crystal hurried to take a shower while thinking about how good it had felt to be with Angel. She had only gotten a chance to feel Angel's fingers between her legs, but she wondered what it would have felt like to feel her tongue instead. That was something they'd both have to find out some other time because right now, they both had a job to go to.

Chapter 13

Friday night, Lickety Splits was filled to capacity. For the first time in the club's history, Barry Licks had to turn customers around at the front door because there were no more seats inside.

Ever since Barry had hired the ten new girls, business has been booming. It was now the strip club that Barry visualized, and because of his keen eye for beauty, he'd finally had what he wanted.

The night was still young, and Billy Brocks was already inside the club. He hadn't expected it to be this crowded, but he wasn't worried because he'd already purchased a private seat in the VIP section of the club. He was hoping to see the exotic-looking dancer that he'd seen the first time he'd come to the club, and although he didn't know exactly what it was that had made her so attractive, he definitely knew that there was something different about her. The way she moved, looked, and swirled her curvaceous hips were all unique; but there was still something mysterious about her. And although he couldn't put his finger on it, it made him want her even more.

Billy watched closely as a tall girl walked out on stage. A slender brunette with a pretty face, but too skinny for Billy's taste. He knew who he'd come to the club to see, and he also knew that he hadn't seen her yet. He began to wonder if the woman he'd seen had even come to work that night. He was already starting on his third beer, and the moment he'd thought about ordering another one, the exotic woman appeared on stage. She was still as beautiful as the first night he'd seen her. Having long, black, curly hair and beautiful golden skin, she was even more exotic than he remembered. Barry had been watching Billy from a table near the back of the club. It was part of his duty to make sure that his VIP guests were as happy and comfortable as possible while attending his club. Barry noticed how Billy had leaned forward in his chair, giving Crystal his undivided attention when she came on stage. He thought that he was on to something, so he immediately sent one of his cocktail waitresses to the dressing room to get Crystal after she'd finished her performance. He asked that she report to the VIP section immediately because there was some possible money to be made. He'd also sent one of his other cocktail waitresses over to Billy's table with two more of the same kind of beer that he'd been drinking before telling him that the beers were on the house. The waitress informed Billy that someone was on her way to do something special for him, and that it too would be on the house. Billy was shocked by the news because he hadn't requested any special attention from anyone. He heard the music come on, so he watched as Angel appeared on stage, but he hadn't seen the girl who'd entered the VIP section through a side door. After entering the dimly lit room, Crystal looked toward the back corner where Barry usually sat. He pointed in the direction of the young man wearing the expensive tailored suit, so Crystal strolled toward the young man's table and began dancing seductively to the same slow song that Angel was on stage dancing to.

Billy was immediately surprised when he glanced up and saw Crystal. The woman was even more beautiful up close, and Billy was shocked because she hadn't wasted any time removing the white thong panties she was wearing.

Crystal noticed that Billy was tense, so she wondered if privacy would help him loosen up. She reached up and drew the curtains closed around them, but continued dancing. The private dances were only one of the several benefits that could be received by the patrons sitting in the VIP section, and Billy was really enjoying himself. Crystal stared directly into his eyes as she moved closer and proceeded to give him a very personal lap dance. Billy began to relax as Crystal turned around and danced with her ass just inches from his face. She bent all the way over in front of him before grinding sexily on his crotch.

Crystal could feel that Billy was really enjoying her performance, so she gently began massaging his chest and shoulders while straddling his lap. She'd done this same routine many times before with a variety of men, but something was different about this man. Crystal couldn't understand what she was feeling or why she was feeling it, but making eye contact with the strange man was beginning to have a strange affect on her. It was the same feeling that she'd felt when she first noticed him sitting in the audience the first night she'd danced at the club. She knew that Billy was the same man that she'd thought about inside the cab on her way home that night, but she had somehow dismissed the idea of ever seeing him again.

Here she was, giving him a lap dance while staring at the burning desire he had in his eyes, and she knew that he was feeling it too.

At the end of the second song, Crystal smiled at Billy and was about to open the curtain when he gently grabbed her arm. "Please stay," he asked in a soft voice.

"I'll stay for a while, but it's against the club's rules to keep the curtains closed once the dance is over," Crystal said while pulling away.

Billy released his grip so that Crystal could open the curtain. He was blown away by her performance, so he didn't want to see her leave. "What's your name?" he asked nervously.

"I'm Crystal. What's yours?"

"You can call me Billy."

"You come here a lot, Billy?"

"This is only my second time. How long have you worked here?"

"Only a week now."

The two had gotten quite comfortable talking to each other before Barry came over to intervene. He introduced himself to Billy as the club's owner before reminding Crystal that she was on the job. Crystal and Billy both stood up before Billy reached into his front pants pocket and removed a wad of cash. Barry walked away as if he was giving them privacy, but was still watching from the corner of his eye as Billy counted out five one-hundred-dollar bills and handed them to Crystal. "Can I see you again?"

"Baby, for this kind of money, you can see me anytime you want," Crystal replied.

"How about tomorrow night?"

"I'll be here," Crystal replied sexily.

"Same time, same place."

After thanking Billy, Crystal gently squeezed his hand before turning and walking out of the same side door that she'd entered through. Billy watched as she made her exit before turning to leave the club himself. He'd already seen what he'd come to see, and Crystal had been all the woman he'd needed to see for one night.

Chapter 14

Early Saturday morning, Billy lie in bed, watching the ceiling fan spin in circles while thinking about Crystal. He'd woken up a few times during the night and imagined her lying in the empty space on the other side of his water bed. Billy had never thought about a woman this much before, so he questioned himself and wondered if he was wrong for thinking about Crystal the way that he was. He got up from his king-size water bed and stumbled to the bathroom to get himself together. He shaved before getting in the shower then realized that he was feeling a lot better than he had in a long time. He decided that he'd treat himself by going out for breakfast instead of preparing it himself. He wasn't craving a drink the way he had on several other mornings, and since he was feeling up to it, he decided on going to the carwash after eating breakfast to wash his SUV. Washing the truck has been on his mind for over a week, so he made plans to finally take care of it. Besides, he and Crystal had made plans to see each other again later that night; and who knows, maybe he'll get lucky? Billy thought.

After taking a long hot shower, Billy opened his closet to figure out what he'd wear for the day. Since he'd planned to wash his Yukon after breakfast, he decided on wearing his Sean John jogging suit and a pair of hiking boots that he'd never worn before. He didn't feel over dressed, but he wondered if he was presentable enough to dine at the upscale restaurant he enjoyed so much. He quickly rid himself of the thought and proceeded to get dressed. Shortly afterward, he was pulling out of the driveway of his upper-class neighborhood in Summerlin. While en route to the restaurant he'd often frequented, Billy floored the accelerator on the Yukon to test its speed. While speeding down the long stretch of highway, his mind once again returned to Crystal. He wondered what else he'd find to do that day because he needed something that'll keep his mind occupied until the time came for he and Crystal to see each other again.

On the other side of town, Crystal had just been brought back to reality when she smelled something burning in the kitchen. She'd been on the sofa watching television when she suddenly remembered that she'd put a few pieces of bacon inside the oven. She quickly jumped off the sofa and hurried to the kitchen before laughing out loud when she saw that the bacon had been burnt to a crisp. She'd been too busy thinking about the man that she'd met the night before. He was still heavy on her mind, and she could still see the look in his eyes when she'd given him the lap dance. She'd hoped to see the man again later on that same night, but he had already left the club by the time her shift had ended. Crystal wondered if the man was married, had a girlfriend, or had children. She realized that she might be jumping the gun on this one because she didn't know anything about the man she was constantly thinking about. All she'd learned was that his name was Billy. She didn't know what he did for a living or if he did anything at all, but he had dressed well and carried himself in a professional manner both times she'd seen him. She wondered if he was some kind of pimp or someone involved in criminal activities. Her mind was everywhere, and she had a bundle of questions with no one to help her answer them. He did say that he wanted to see her again, so when the time came, she planned to get answers to all of her questions.

Crystal tossed the burnt bacon inside the trash and decided on frying a couple of eggs instead. She still had to take a shower, but decided on doing that after straightening up her room a little. Her mind began to drift again, but this time, she reminisced about her experience with Angel. Although she did enjoy the time they'd spent together, Crystal preferred that her next sexual encounter be with Billy.

Chapter 15

Saturday night, Lickety Splits was as packed as it had been the night before. Billy was already sitting at his table in the VIP section at eight o'clock. Crystal wasn't scheduled to go on stage until eight thirty, so she decided to peek through the side door of the VIP section to see if Billy was inside. To her surprise, he was; and since she still had a half-hour before starting her shift, she decided to pay Billy a surprise visit before the show. "Hey, handsome," she said while approaching his table.

"Hey, babe, it's good to see you," he replied happily.

Crystal continued to smile while sitting across from Billy. "Well, Billy, since you already know what my job is, may I ask what you do for a living?" Crystal asked suddenly.

"I'm a lawyer."

"A lawyer? Bullshit!"

After reaching for the wallet that was located in his back pocket, Billy flipped it open and removed one of his business cards before handing it to Crystal. "Billy Brocks, attorney at law," she said while reading out loud.

"And that would be me," Billy said with a smile.

"Brocks & Brocks Law Offices. Does that mean you own it?"

"My father and grandfather founded it, but I inherited part of it when they passed away," he said while staring at the floor.

Crystal didn't want to ask how the men had died, so she avoided the topic altogether. She was impressed with Billy, and she couldn't believe that she'd actually met a lawyer, especially one who's as young and good-looking as Billy. "Are you married?" Crystal asked.

"No wife, no kids," Billy answered.

"I guess that makes you a good catch?" Crystal asked while smiling.

"I guess you could say that. What about you?"

"I'm also single with no children," Crystal replied softly.

As their eyes locked on each other, they both knew what the near future had in store for them. They continued to discuss a variety of topics in which they spoke openly and honestly. Billy shared his pending legal troubles, and Crystal was surprised to hear that lawyers experienced problems just like everybody else. She hoped his situation would turn out okay because she really enjoyed his company. Billy learned that Crystal was from Atlanta and had recently moved to Las Vegas to start a new life. He also learned that she didn't have a family because she'd been placed in foster care at a young age. He wanted to ease his curiosity, so he asked Crystal about her nationality. He learned she was a mixture of black and Asian, which he had no problem with. "Well, it's about time for my shift to start," she said while glancing at her watch.

"I'll be here waiting for my lap dance," Billy replied jokingly.

"I'll come back when I can," Crystal said while handing the business card back to Billy.

"No, keep it and give me a call sometime."

"Enjoy the show," she said before turning to leave.

Once inside the dressing room, Crystal placed Billy's business card inside her purse with hopes of calling him real soon.

Moments later, she was being introduced to come out on stage. Crystal had quickly become one of the main attractions at Lickety Splits. Several of the male patrons had made comments to Barry that Crystal was the only reason they'd came to the club.

Billy sat in VIP sipping his beer as Crystal walked out on stage. Most of the lights inside the club were turned off, but an array of colorful stage lights remained on. Billy was proud of the fact that he'd met Crystal, because not only was she beautiful, but she had the personality to go with it. She'd been very easy to talk to, and Billy could definitely use somebody to talk to these days.

As the lights continued to shine bright, Crystal glanced up to make sure Billy was watching. She'd just finished stripping down naked and was about to begin her dance routine when she suddenly became dizzy. Crystal was still dancing to her first song, and she worried that she wouldn't make it through the next one.

Billy was watching closely from the VIP section when he noticed that something was wrong. Crystal stumbled a few times, and it appeared that she was having trouble with keeping her balance because her entire body seemed to be moving in slow motion while she stared aimlessly at the floor. Barry had also been watching Crystal from across the room, but he thought that she was trying out a new routine. The stage lights became terribly bright, and the music was blaring to the point where Crystal could no longer understand the words or figure out what song was being played. She'd suddenly stopped moving altogether while trying to regain her composure before suddenly collapsing on stage. Several people had to be restrained by the club's bouncers as they desperately tried to climb on stage to come to Crystal's aid. Barry ran and jumped on stage before kneeling down beside Crystal. He was extremely frightened, so he fanned her face with his hand in a desperate attempt to cool her off. He guarded Crystal by hovering over her body and making sure that no one else could get close. She was sweating profusely, so Barry used the handkerchief that he kept in his back pocket to wipe the sweat from Crystal's face and forehead.

Angel immediately ran out from the dressing room when she heard the commotion. She didn't know what to think when she saw Crystal sprawled out on stage with Barry hovering over her. "Crystal!" Angel yelled.

Angel was too scared to approach, so she stood there crying while searching the room in hopes of finding her boyfriend Frank. Frank was also in disbelief. He's one of the club's bouncers, but he was also scared because he had gotten to know Crystal pretty well through his girlfriend Angel. The two girls had become inseparable, so he knew that the situation would be too much for Angel to handle. He noticed Angel standing completely frozen by the stage's exit before rushing to her side. Frank held her head closely to his chest as they both looked at Crystal with tears in their eyes. Billy couldn't believe what he'd seen. He was so terrified that he'd already dialed 911 from his cell phone before making his way from the VIP section. He had just gotten better acquainted with her right before she'd gone on stage. She seemed fine when they'd talked, so he didn't understand what could have possibly gone wrong in only a few minutes. Billy was hoping that she'd be fine because he really looked forward to spending more time with her.

A few hours later, Crystal woke up in the emergency room at University Medical Center. She didn't know what had happened, but she did remember getting dizzy while dancing on stage.

An elderly nurse had been assigned to watch Crystal's progress, so she was very happy to see Crystal awake. "How are you feeling, hon?" the nurse asked in a concerned voice.

"What happened?"

"You were rushed here by the ambulance after collapsing at your job. You have a few friends outside who have been waiting to see you, would you like for me to let them in?"

"Sure," Crystal answered in a voice that was barely audible.

Moments later, Crystal smiled when she saw Angel running toward her. "Hey, girl, are you all right?" Angel asked.

"I don't even remember what happened," Crystal replied.

Her smile got even bigger when she saw the other people that were there to see her. "Don't do that to us no more, Crystal. You scared us," Frank said with a smile.

Crystal had still been smiling from Frank's remark when Barry approached, "How are you?"

"I'm fine, but I still don't know what happened," she said while looking at her boss.

"We don't know what happened either, so I'm giving you some time off to allow you to rest up."

Everybody watched as Billy slowly approached Crystal's bedside, holding a single red rose in his hand. After handing her the rose, he kissed her gently on the cheek as his eyes began to fill with water, "Get well, beautiful," he said in a caring voice.

"Thanks for coming," she replied before raising her arms to give him a hug.

"The doctor said you're dehydrated," Billy said loud enough so that everyone in the room could hear. "He also said that you'll be fine as long as you drink lots of fluids and get plenty of rest."

As soon as Billy had finished talking, the doctor entered the room. "Hi, I'm Dr. Chaps. Ms. Tradwell, you collapsed because your body could no longer function after suffering from dehydration. Your body lacks the fluids and nutrients that it needs. I don't feel it's necessary to run tests or waste anyone's time because this happens to strippers all the time," the doctor said while staring at Crystal.

Billy thought that the doctor's remark had come very inappropriately, but since he was out of his field, he decided not to comment.

Chapter 16

A month after being discharged from the hospital, Crystal has been trying her best to take it easy. Since Dr. Chaps had said she was dehydrated, she'd taken his advice by consuming lots of water and fruit juices. She still felt herself getting dizzy for no reason from time to time, and because of that, she hasn't been back to work but still managed to talk to Angel every day.

Barry advised Crystal to take as much time off as she needed, and her job would still be waiting for her whenever she decides to return. He said he wanted to make sure that she was healthy and feeling well before he'd allow her to come back.

Crystal and Billy were seeing each other daily. They've been growing a lot closer but taking things very slowly. They were basically just enjoying each other's company since Crystal had made it clear that she wasn't ready to get intimate quite yet. Billy was trying not to pressure her too much, but he sometimes found it hard not to.

A couple of weeks after Crystal was released from the hospital, Billy had asked to spend some time with her. He picked her up early one morning and took her on a long drive to the Hoover Dam. Crystal enjoyed the trip so much that she'd begged him to take her back again as soon as possible. He'd promised to take her somewhere different on the coming weekend, and she is really looking forward to it.

Billy has been extremely busy at work for the past week, and it hadn't taken Simone long to notice the change. She'd recognized the difference in his attitude, but didn't want to appear to be nosy by asking why he'd been so happy. Billy has been acting like his normal self again, so Simone was very pleased to see the change. He'd even been showing up early at the office and taking care of business the way he once had. Instead of the strong smell of alcohol all over his breath and clothes, Simone smelled the sweet scent of expensive cologne. Billy had again begun shaving on a daily basis and dressing immaculately like he used to before the courtroom incident. Simone was optimistic and certain that everything would be back to normal once his sentencing was over with. He'd still have to be sanctioned by the bar association, but she wasn't worried about that. Billy had just won an appeal for a client who'd been in prison for twelve years. He's now in search of an attorney who'd be willing to represent his client in court. Since being barred from making courtroom appearances, Billy has been frustrated because he knows that he could win a lot of his cases.

His client has been granted a new trial, and there's a pile of paperwork to be reviewed. Billy is already familiar with all the documents and pleadings on file, and it's going to take a new attorney even more time to read everything, which means that his client, Richie Callis, is going to have to wait even longer than the twelve years he's already served to see justice in his case.

Richie was very upset after Billy arranged a visit to explain the situation. He explained that he'd done everything in his power to better Richie's predicament, but everything he'd tried had failed.

Chapter 17

Billy was excited about picking Crystal up from her room. He'd planned something special for the weekend, and he hoped she'd accept it well. The rain fell hard as he carefully crossed the railroad tracks, but since he was so anxious to start the day, he drove as fast as he could without losing control of the large SUV. He still had a stop to make before picking Crystal up, so he swung the Yukon around a corner and almost brought it to a complete stop before pulling into the parking lot of a floral shop. He didn't plan to stay long, so he kept the truck's engine running with the windshield wipers on low speed while he ran inside.

Shortly afterward, he returned to the SUV carrying two dozen long-stemmed red roses. He'd promised Crystal something very special, and although she'd pressed for details, he still hadn't told her what it was.

After running his errands, Billy headed for the Budget Suites to pick Crystal up. They'd spent a lot of time together over the past few weeks, and he still wasn't sure about the status of their relationship. He wasn't clear about whether he should consider her as his girlfriend or only as a friend, so he began to have doubts about his current plans.

Billy wasn't sure how Crystal was going to react to what he'd planned, but the moment he pulled into the parking lot of the Budget Suites, all doubts were erased from his mind. He pulled the large Yukon directly in front of Crystal's room, and instead of honking the horn, he quickly exited the truck and shielded himself from the falling rain while running toward her room door. The moment he knocked on the door, Crystal snatched it open as if she'd been standing there waiting for someone to knock on it. "Hi, babe," Billy said nervously.

"Hey, sweetheart," Crystal replied.

Billy leaned forward and kissed her gently on the cheek while handing her the two dozen roses. "Thank you," she said while sniffing them.

"No problem. Are you ready?"

"Yes, but give me a minute to put these in some water."

Billy waited outside while she put the roses in some water before grabbing her purse and jacket. After locking the door, she took hold of his arm and ran with him toward the passenger side of the nearby SUV. Billy did what he could to shield Crystal from the falling rain, but since neither had brought an umbrella, she'd still gotten a little wet. He helped as she climbed into the passenger side of the large truck, but once she was safely inside, he ran around the back before climbing in on the driver's side. Billy put the truck in reverse before glancing at Crystal and watched her as she listened to the rain fall noisily on the windshield. He turned on the truck's windshield wipers, and she watched as they removed the rain just as quickly as it fell. "Where are we going?" she asked curiously.

"It wouldn't be a surprise if I told you now, would it?" Billy replied sarcastically. He'd felt completely at ease and was really looking forward to spending the day with Crystal.

It was late afternoon, but Billy knew what he'd planned would take all day. It appeared to be later than it actually was because the dark clouds have formed in the sky while it rained. He'd thought that the timing was perfect because the stormy weather would give him a reason to cuddle with Crystal. And since romance was part of the plan, what better weather could he ask for? he thought.

As they cruised along the highway, Billy turned on the radio to the station that Crystal enjoyed listening to. It played back-to-back love songs, and he listened closely as she sung most of the words. "You're still not gonna tell me where we're going?" Crystal asked.

"You'll know when we get there," Billy answered calmly.

After thirty minutes of riding, Crystal raised from her reclined position after Billy glanced at her from the corner of his eye. She'd gotten so relaxed and into her music that she'd stopped paying attention to where they were headed. Crystal read the sign as Billy made a left turn down what appeared to be another long road. The sign read Mount Charleston, so she became more curious than she'd been before. "Now what are we going to do at this mountain?"

"All I can tell you is that we won't be hiking," Billy replied.

As the SUV continued to travel up the long road, the radio station began to fade in and out. They were beginning to lose the signal, and the sound became agitating, so Crystal reached over and turned it off. While gazing at the hills ahead, she felt that the climate had changed. Her ears were plugged up, and she had to swallow a few times to unplug them. She no longer heard the rain falling on the windshield, but she still saw something falling from the sky. "Is that snow?" she asked while rolling down the passenger side window.

"Yep, that's what it is," Billy replied while focusing on the road. By him being from Las Vegas, he knew that it was possible for it to be snowing at Mount Charleston. As they entered the hills, Billy slowed down the SUV because he knew that there were curves and dips in the road ahead. As Crystal watched the snow get thicker, she still didn't know what to expect. She just hoped that the SUV would be able to handle the slippery road. While staring ahead, she spotted what she thought was a large building but couldn't make out what it was. As they got closer, it appeared to be a large motel, but she couldn't figure out why a motel would be built in the middle of the mountains. When they'd finally reached the building, Crystal read the sign out loud, "Mount Charleston Lodge."

Billy didn't respond; he just proceeded to find a parking space large enough for the SUV. Crystal still didn't know what they would be doing once she'd climbed out of the large vehicle, so she played with the falling snowflakes while walking toward the lodge. As soon as they entered the building, she stopped immediately. "This is beautiful," she said while looking around. "Are those real?" she asked while pointing at the large animal heads mounted on the walls.

"Yes, they're real," Billy replied.

After a moment of allowing her to look around, Billy reached for Crystal's hand and placed his arm around her waist before guiding her toward an elegant restaurant that he'd frequented a few times in the past. As they walked toward the restaurant, Crystal read a sign before realizing why she'd mistaken the lodge to be a large motel. The building had several rooms inside with a pair of fancy looking elevators that went to all the different floors. She quickly ignored the eye-catching elevators the moment Billy tugged lightly on her arm, pulling her closer to him.

After arriving at the restaurant, Billy informed the cashier that he'd made reservations the day before. The cashier easily confirmed the information by looking his name up in a log that was kept near the telephone. Moments later, while the hostess was escorting them to their table, Billy glanced at Crystal and smiled as she stared directly into his eyes. Once they'd been seated at the table for two, Billy gazed across the table and still found himself fascinated by Crystal's beauty. "We have all day, so there won't be any need to rush," he said before continuing, "I've also made reservations for us to spend the night out here."

"Are you serious? You devil!" Crystal replied while smiling.

She didn't appear to be offended by what he'd planned without her consent, so Billy was relieved once he'd gotten that out of the way.

A short while later, a waiter came out to take their order. He was a short Hispanic man that wore a long, but well-groomed, mustache. Crystal allowed Billy to order for the both of them since he'd been the one who'd planned everything else. The waiter returned to their table carrying the beverages they'd ordered along with a couple of empty wine glasses for the expensive champagne Billy ordered. He popped the cork for the attractive couple and told them to enjoy before leaving the table.

While Billy poured champagne in both of their glasses, Crystal slid closer toward him before holding up her glass and proposing a toast. "To a wonderful evening," Billy said.

"To us," Crystal replied while leaning forward and kissing him softly on the lips.

Moments later, the waiter was back at their table. This time, he'd brought along another waiter who helped him carry one of the trays that contained their food. He gently sat the steak and lobster on the table in front of Crystal along with a variety of condiments. "Enjoy your meal and the rest of the evening," he said politely before leaving.

After they'd finished their meal, Billy sat closely with his arm around Crystal. They were stuffed, so they sat and enjoyed a little small talk while sipping the last of their champagne. The champagne had begun to take its affect as they laughed and giggled about how delicious the food had been.

As the soft music played throughout the dimly lit restaurant, Crystal and Billy had both became aroused. Everything was going wonderfully, so she thanked him with another soft kiss for being there and making her feel special. She'd never had a man to do all the sweet things for her that Billy had done since they'd met. The two felt really compatible with each other because they had a lot of things in common: neither of them had ever been married, had children, or had a family since at a very young age. They'd become extremely comfortable around each other, and Crystal wondered if Billy would be the man that she would finally settle down with. Although she had no way of knowing, but Billy had also been wondering the same thing about her. They'd finally decided to get up and leave the restaurant after sitting there for well over two hours. Billy left the waiter a fifty-dollar tip because not only was the food delicious, but he'd appreciated the waiter for bringing everything they would need at once instead of having to keep interrupting he and Crystal. The two walked slowly together outside the restaurant after Billy paid the bill. Since Crystal didn't know where to go, she stayed at Billy's side and allowed him to lead the way. They entered a gift shop before leaving the lodge. After a few minutes of browsing around, Billy handed Crystal his visa and allowed her to buy whatever she wanted. He excused himself to go to the restroom while leaving Crystal inside the gift shop. When he exited the restroom, he was surprised to see that Crystal was already standing there waiting for him and holding two bags. She smiled with a sexy look in her eyes, but Billy didn't question her. He just reached out and grabbed the credit card that she'd been trying to hand back to him. "I bought something for both of us," she said sexily.

"What is it?" Billy asked.

"It wouldn't be a surprise if I told you now, would it?" she asked before laughing out loud.

Billy laughed in return as he heard the same exact words that he'd said to her earlier. "Let's go get our room," he said while glancing at his watch.

The evening was winding down quickly, so Billy thought that it would be best if they settled in for the night. When they began walking, Crystal headed in one direction while Billy headed in another. He smiled when he noticed that Crystal was headed in the direction of the elevators. "Where are you going?" she asked.

"We have to drive where I'm going."

"I thought you said we already had reservations to stay here for the night?"

"We do, but not for the lodge," Billy replied.

"You're confusing me."

"You'll see when we get there," he said while placing his arm around Crystal's waist and heading toward the exit.

A short distance from the lodge, Billy pulled into an area that contained about a dozen small cabins. "Are we staying here?" Crystal asked with excitement.

"Yep, one is ours for the night," Billy replied while wiggling the key in front of her.

As he parked in front of the cabin, he reached into the backseat of the spacious SUV and grabbed a bag that contained a couple of bottles of wine that he'd bought. At the same moment, Crystal reached under the passenger's side seat and pulled out the two bags containing the items she'd purchased at the gift shop.

When they entered the cabin and closed the door behind them, Crystal was stunned. The cabin was fully furnished and included an entertainment center along with a large fireplace. The setting was extremely romantic, and Crystal was really beginning to look forward to spending the night with Billy.

They began getting comfortable by removing their jackets and hanging them up on a small coatrack that was located near the front door. Billy picked up the nearby remote control before switching on the television and the stereo. He quickly located the radio station that Crystal enjoyed, and although the signal had gotten weak inside the SUV, it played clearly on the cabin's stereo.

Crystal went to the bathroom and was surprised to see that it had a large hot tub inside. She immediately got it started before removing her clothes to get inside. "Billy, come in here!" she yelled.

When the door swung open, Billy smiled when he saw that Crystal was naked and inside the hot tub. "Get in with me," she said while patting the empty space beside her.

Billy jumped at the opportunity, but before he joined her, he held up his index finger indicating that he'd be back in a minute. When he returned, he held up two wine glasses and a bottle of the red wine that he'd brought along.

After sitting down the bottle and handing Crystal the wine glasses, he hesitated while staring at the floor. Crystal noticed his hesitation, so she stood up, exposing her beautiful breasts and erect nipples along with the rest of her curvaceous body. Billy was nervous because he'd met Crystal at a strip club, and although he'd seen her naked on many occasions, she'd never seen him, and he wasn't sure how she would react after seeing his body.

She watched closely as he removed his T-shirt and began unbuttoning his pants. Billy was still nervous, so she grabbed his arm and pulled him closer before kissing him passionately. She continued to kiss him in a way that she'd never kissed him before, but it was something they'd both been wanting. She wanted him to feel more comfortable, so she began to rub all over his chest and back. She broke the kiss while massaging his shoulders and sucking the left side of his neck. Billy was immediately turned on, so he kicked off his shoes and allowed his pants to fall to the floor. He stood wearing only his underwear, so Crystal sat inside the hot tub and watched as he pulled them off before climbing inside and sitting beside her. They began kissing wild and passionately before Billy went down to kiss Crystal's breasts. He sucked each nipple slowly, but thoroughly until Crystal began to arch her back. She held his head firmly against her breast as Billy continued to lick each nipple back and forth. Suddenly, she stood up from the water before sitting on the edge of the hot tub. As Billy kissed his way toward her flat stomach, she watched as he licked slowly around her belly button before spreading her legs wide enough for his head to fit in between. Billy was in a daze. He'd fantasized many times about being with Crystal, and now his fantasy had finally come true. He kissed her inner thighs before licking back and forth on her lubricated slit. Crystal opened her legs even wider, so Billy took advantage by parting her labia with his thumbs before licking slowly on her protruding clit. Crystal closed her eyes and moaned softly while enjoying Billy's warm tongue. It had been a long time since anyone had licked her special spot, so Crystal tried her best to enjoy the moment. She tried to remember the last time she'd felt so good until her body began shaking as she reached orgasm.

As Billy continued to lick her special spot, Crystal gently pushed him back before lowering her legs. She stood him in front of her before kneeling down and taking his manhood inside her mouth. Billy closed his eyes and moaned softly as Crystal sucked his manhood with expertise. Although many women had done it many times before, Billy couldn't remember ever having it done like this. Crystal stayed on her knees and continued to bob her head back and forth until his entire body began to stiffen. He tried pulling back, but she resisted and continued to suck his manhood until he ejaculated.

With both legs now weakened, Billy sat inside the hot tub with his arm around Crystal. He tried catching his breath while she stared at him to see if he'd enjoyed what she'd just given him. "Geez!" he said while wiping the sweat from his forehead.

Crystal smiled because that was all he'd been able to say after her excellent performance. She scooted closer while handing him a glass and filling it with wine. As they talked and drank wine, they held each other closely while Billy tried mustering more energy. The two made love for the first time that night, trying different positions in different parts of the cabin until they finally passed out on the bed from exhaustion.

Chapter 18

The following morning, Crystal and Billy were still naked, so they made love again before leaving the cabin. They'd enjoyed a wonderful night together, and love was definitely in the air.

After returning the cabin key to the main office, they held each other closely as they prepared to travel the long stretch of highway back to Las Vegas. Crystal never did get the chance to put on the sexy lingerie that she'd purchased from the gift shop the evening before, but she figured she would have plenty of opportunities to do that. She'd also have to wait to see Billy wear what she'd bought for him. *Oh well, there will be other times,* she thought.

On the way home, Billy promised that he'd stop somewhere so they could eat breakfast. Crystal liked the idea because she was hungry and beginning to feel nauseous. She didn't know if it was from all the sex they'd had or from all the wine she'd drank the night before. She told Billy that she wasn't feeling too good before scooting away and closing her eyes for a while. He understood, so he drove in silence until they reached the restaurant where they hoped to have breakfast.

Billy had really begun to have feelings for Crystal. He knew that she was special because he'd never felt connected to any woman the way he felt connected to Crystal. And although he'd met her at a strip club, he didn't view her in a degrading fashion. To Billy, she was just a beautiful young woman who did what she had to in order to survive. Not only that, but Crystal was different. He'd never had to wait more than a few days to sleep with any woman, but Crystal had made him wait for nearly a month before sleeping with him.

Since Crystal wasn't feeling well, Billy thought that maybe he should take her back to his home in Summerlin after eating breakfast. He didn't want to make the decision without her consent, so he decided he'd wait to see how she'd feel about it. After glancing in her direction, he watched for a while as she lay with her head fitted comfortably between the seat and the door of the SUV. And although her eyes were closed, Crystal was still as beautiful as ever, and Billy was extremely proud to be in her company. From the moment they'd met, he wondered if he'd ever get the chance to sleep with her. But now that he had, he realized that the experience had been far greater than he could have ever imagined. When it came to lovemaking, Crystal's performance had surpassed every woman he'd ever been with. Her style and technique had been one that he'd never come across before, and for that reason, he wondered how she'd acquired the skills that seemed well beyond her years.

After entering the restaurant's parking lot, Crystal wasn't feeling any better. "I don't feel like going inside, Billy, don't they have a drive-thru?" she asked in frustration.

"Nice restaurants usually don't have a drive-thru, but if you'd like, I could find somewhere that does."

"I'd appreciate it," she replied in a tired voice.

Billy found a drive-thru less than a block away. It was at a local McDonalds, but as Billy recalled, McDonalds had a nice breakfast menu. Instead of bothering Crystal a second time, he ordered for the both of them the way he'd done at the lodge the evening before. He ordered some pancakes, scrambled eggs, sausages, and a couple of large glasses of orange juice. After he'd paid for the meal, Billy headed for his home in Summerlin. He'd changed his mind about asking Crystal what she wanted to do. It appeared that they were officially a couple, so Billy wanted to be by his woman's side to make sure she'd be okay.

Chapter 19

"Mr. Brocks, you have a call on line 1," Simone said softly over the intercom.

"This is Mr. Brocks, what can I do for you?"

"Hi, babe."

"Oh hi, sweetheart. How are you?"

"I'm fine, but I'll be even better when you get home," Crystal replied.

"I'll be there as soon as I can," Billy said while glancing at his watch.

"Okay, babe, I just wanted to hear your voice because I miss you."

"I miss you too, sweetheart, and I'll see you soon," Billy said before hanging up.

Billy knew that he'd fallen in love with Crystal. She often called him at his job only to say that she missed him, and he really enjoyed it because no other woman had ever done that before. Billy's sentencing date was approaching, but he wasn't worried about it. His mind was on Crystal, and she was all he'd allowed himself to think about. He thought about her constantly, and it soon became hard for him to focus on his job.

Crystal still had a room at the Budget Suites, but she hadn't been staying there at all lately. She hasn't even talked to Angel in a while, but as far as she knew, they were still friends. Since she and Billy had gotten together, Crystal had barely had time for anybody because they were doing everything together. After the Mount Charleston weekend, Crystal and Billy had gone to a carnival that was only in town for a couple of days. Billy had always been terrified of heights, but Crystal managed to talk him into riding everything she rode. After riding the roller coaster, the Ferris wheel, and the zipper, Billy was nauseated; but he continued to do whatever Crystal asked of him. She was some kind of woman, and he was loving everything about her so far. Since she was often at his home in Summerlin, Billy had given her a set of keys to his BMW, which allowed her to run errands while he was at work. That was his way of helping her out so that she wouldn't have to call cabs or wait on bus stops while he was away. After all, she'd also been helping him out in a lot of ways. Crystal would clean house on a daily basis, wash and fold his laundry, and she'd always taken care of his sexual needs whenever they were together. The two were really enjoying each other, and Billy was a much happier man when Crystal was around. Most of the time, they would just stay home and cuddle on the couch while watching a movie. Crystal still hadn't gone back to Lickety Splits since collapsing on stage, and she didn't know when she would be going back. She hoped that it would be soon, but Billy thinks that she should wait a while longer since she still get sick at times. He'd offered several times to take her back to the doctor, but she insisted she'd be fine after taking some aspirin and lying down for a while.

Sitting at his desk, Billy glanced at his watch a few times to check the time. He was always in a hurry to leave the office after being there for only a few hours. Simone had become very suspicious of Billy's activities, because a few times when he'd left the office early, he'd told her that he was going over to the county jail to visit a client; but on a few occasions, the client that he was supposed to be visiting had called the office looking for him. When asked if Billy had been to visit, the client would always answer that he hadn't. Simone had never questioned her boss's whereabouts before, but she was beginning to suspect that he was up to no good. And although she didn't know exactly what it was, she'd become very tempted to find out.

Chapter 20

Michael Shoemaker had just flown in from San Francisco before he and Billy met in the lobby of Brocks & Brocks. They discussed worst-case scenarios of what could possibly happen when Billy would be sentenced in a few hours. Things had not gone according to plan, and Mr. Shoemaker was very concerned about the possible sentence that Billy could receive. Instead of pleading to a misdemeanor simple assault, Billy had pled to a felony assault. The felony conviction could easily land him in prison, so it would be left to Michael Shoemaker to argue probation as opposed to the harsher punishment that the district attorney would be arguing for.

After spending more than two hours discussing the issue, Billy and his attorney left the lobby and headed to court. It was only a short distance between Brocks & Brocks and the courthouse, so the two men arrived in less than five minutes. Billy was nervous as he entered the courtroom. As soon as he was inside, he quickly noticed that the district attorney he'd assaulted was already inside and watching the door as people entered. Philip Doolittle glanced at Billy, but as soon as they'd made eye contact, he averted his eyes to another direction. Billy hadn't known what to think, but it did make him extremely uncomfortable.

After everyone had taken their seats, the bailiff entered the courtroom from the judge's chambers and asked that everyone rise as the judge made his entrance. Immediately after the judge had taken his seat behind the bench, the district attorney stood up to inform the court that an attorney was present from San Francisco representing Billy Brocks. He stated that if the court didn't mind,

Chapter 21

Billy had only been at the office for a few hours before deciding to call it a day. He'd just been sentenced to three years of probation and ordered to pay a ten-thousand-dollar fine for assaulting Philip Doolittle. He was extremely upset about the sentence, so he contemplated on whether or not he should appeal it. He'd still have to be sanctioned by the bar association, and since his sentencing was now resolved, they would be conducting their own investigation of his alleged misconduct. He still didn't understand why an investigation would be necessary since he'd already pled guilty to assault. He figured that it would only be a waste of time trying to speculate about the matter since he had no control over it.

The weather was nice, and since he didn't feel like going home at the moment, Billy weaved the large Yukon in and out of traffic while trying to figure out what he wanted to do. He needed to vent, and he wanted to go somewhere and do it in private, but he also wanted to spend time with Crystal.

Billy decided on a long drive because he thought that maybe it would help take his mind off the sentence he'd just received. He was still confused and didn't know what to think about everything that had just happened. He wasn't even sure if he could do three years successfully on probation, but if he couldn't, he would have to face the consequences of spending five years in prison. The thought of being on probation really bothered Billy. That meant that someone could come to his home unannounced and search his property whenever they felt like it. He'd have someone to report to, and he'd have to submit to random drug tests. *That's how criminals are treated, not attorneys,* Billy thought.

he would like to call Mr. Brocks's case first so that his attorney, Mr. Shoemaker, could be on his way back to California as soon as possible.

After sorting through a stack of files that sat before him, Judge Oram finally spoke. "The *State of Nevada v. Billy Brocks*," he said before continuing. "This is a matter of sentencing for an assault that the defendant has already pled guilty to. I assume that the victim in this case, Philip Doolittle, is here and prepared to testify before I impose sentencing on Mr. Brocks, is that correct?"

"That is correct, Your Honor," the district attorney blurted out.

Judge Oram allowed Philip Doolittle to give his testimony as to what had happened on the morning that he was assaulted by Billy Brocks. After the breathtaking testimony, the entire courtroom appeared to be in shock while staring directly at Billy. They stared at him as if they hated him with all the hatred in the world. Judge Oram had witnessed the incident himself, but he'd still turned red in the face after hearing Philip Doolittle retell his story. "Mr. Brocks, do you have anything to say before this court imposes its sentence against you?" the judge asked angrily.

"Yes, I do, Your Honor. This entire incident was a total accident, and I truly apologize to Mr. Doolittle for allowing my temper to get the best of me," Billy pleaded.

"Mr. Brocks, does this kind of rage run in your family?"

"I don't understand your question, Judge."

"Well, Mr. Brocks, your father and grandfather were both known for their tempers also," the judge said as a matter of fact.

Billy stood in court with a dazed look on his face. That's when Michael Shoemaker spoke up, "Your Honor, Billy's father and grandfather has passed away long before now, and neither man has anything to do with your case against Billy Brocks."

"The *State of Nevada v. Billy Brocks*, I hereby sentences you, Billy Brocks, to five years in state prison to be suspended after serving three years of supervised probation, plus a fine in the amount of ten thousand dollars to be paid in cash to the victim, Philip Doolittle," Judge Oram said angrily before slamming his gavel and calling the next case.

Billy was stunned. He was still standing at the defense table when the attorney for the next case walked up. Mr. Shoemaker was also in disbelief, so he escorted Billy quickly out of the courtroom with his arm around his shoulders. Although they had discussed worst-case scenarios before going to court that morning, Billy and his attorney were both caught off guard by Judge Oram's conduct. The judge seemed to have taken a personal interest in Billy's case instead of handling the case in a professional manner. Billy was told by the bailiff before leaving the courtroom that he needed to report to the office of Parole and Probation before the week was out.

For a moment, Billy thought about stopping at a liquor store and buying something strong enough to make him forget about all of his current problems, but he reached for his cell phone instead. "Hello," Crystal answered sexily.

"Hi, babe."

"Oh, hi. What's going on?"

"I'm on my way home, and I need you to get dressed."

"For what?" Crystal asked.

"I need to talk, but I don't feel like coming inside when I get there," he said in a tired voice.

"How do I need to be dressed?"

"You can wear anything."

"All right, I'll be dressed by the time you get here," Crystal said before hanging up.

Billy arrived at his home within ten minutes after hanging up the phone with Crystal. When he pulled up, he didn't have to honk his horn because Crystal had been looking for him to pull up through the large living room window. She ran out of the house and stopped to lock the front door with the key that Billy had given her, wearing a short blue denim skirt with a small blue halter top that exposed her ample cleavage. She was also carrying an expensive designer handbag that Billy had given her as a gift.

After locking the front door, Billy watched as Crystal tiptoed across the lawn toward the SUV. When she opened the door to climb inside, he caught a quick glimpse of her red panties as she sat down. "Hi, babe," she said while leaning over to give him a kiss.

"Hi, sweetheart, you look nice."

"Thank you," Crystal replied.

At first, Billy hadn't known where he and Crystal were going, but he'd made up his mind the moment she entered the vehicle. Since Crystal enjoyed being around water, he decided on taking her to Lake Mead. It's attached to Hoover Dam, and she'd loved it when he took her there the first time.

On their way to the lake, Billy made a couple of stops to buy him and Crystal something to eat. He bought a bucket of chicken, a twelve-pack of beer, and a case of bottled water so they'd have something to drink along the way. The entire time they'd been riding, Billy had been explaining to Crystal about what had taken place in court that morning. He'd begun to get mad all over again as he recalled how Judge Oram had treated him. "I've always been respected by all the judges since being a lawyer, but now they're treating me like they don't even know me," Billy said in frustration.

"Don't allow them to get to you like that, babe. Things will get better," Crystal said sincerely.

Billy knew that if things were going to get better, they'd better start soon because he was experiencing something that he'd never had to experience before. He hadn't been able to get any new clients since the courtroom incident, and since he'd been ordered to stay out of all courtrooms, he had to refund fifteen thousand dollars back to the clients who'd hired him before the incident took place. Now he'd have to pay ten thousand in fines to the district attorney he'd assaulted.

Billy was now experiencing financial problems, and he wasn't sure how to deal with it because he'd never had to deal with it before. Crystal could see that things were really bothering him, so she slid over and leaned her head against his shoulder while gently rubbing his chest. Her hand was soon inside his pants, so Billy pulled the SUV inside an empty rest area and parked under a shade tree. He turned and kissed Crystal passionately while massaging her breasts. "I love you, Crystal," he said while kissing her neck.

Crystal was still trying to digest what she'd just heard because not only had Billy never said he loved her, but no man had ever told her that before. Billy was shocked at himself because saying he loved Crystal had come so naturally, and he'd never said that to any woman before.

Crystal's eyes began to water as she looked Billy in the eyes before saying, "I love you too."

The two kissed passionately while Crystal pulled Billy's legs from under the steering wheel. After pulling his body to the middle of the seat, she unbuttoned his shirt and began kissing all over his chest and stomach. She unlatched his belt and unbuttoned his pants before carefully pulling his penis through the pee hole of his black silk boxers. Crystal glanced sexily at Billy before going down and devouring his manhood. He still couldn't believe how good she was, and although she'd done it many times before, he still had not asked how she'd gotten so good. As Crystal swallowed every inch of his manhood, Billy pulled her skirt up to her waist before sliding two fingers inside of her from the back. It turned him on even more when he felt how wet she was, and Crystal moaned softly as she continued to suck his manhood in a smooth rhythm.

Billy continued to thrust his fingers in and out of her slippery hole until he felt himself about to ejaculate. His hips began to jerk wildly as he and Crystal both reached orgasm. She licked him clean as always before placing his manhood back inside his pants as if nothing had ever happened. She smiled while staring at Billy because she knew that he loved oral gratification, but she also knew that she drained him every time. Billy leaned his head against the back window of the

SUV, so Crystal laid her head against his chest before repeating that she loved him. "I love you too, and you know I love that," Billy said while smiling.

"Well, they say that practice makes perfect," Crystal replied.

"And how much practice have you had?"

"Lots."

Billy was paying close attention to what Crystal was saying, and he was becoming very upset by her comments. "What do you mean by lots?"

"Several times a day for several years," she replied.

"What? With who?"

"I've already told you that I came to Las Vegas to change my life, Billy."

"Change your life from what?"

"I was homeless and on the streets at a very young age, so I had to sell my body to survive!"

"Oh my god, a prostitute?"

"Is that what you want to hear me say?" Crystal asked.

"For Christ's sake, Crystal, I'm an attorney. I can't be involved in a relationship with a whore!"

"You just said you love me, now you're calling me a whore," Crystal said with tears streaming down her face.

Billy couldn't believe what he was hearing and didn't want to believe that he'd been treating a prostitute like she was something special. This was too much, he thought to himself. He'd just been sentenced hours earlier, now he finds out that the woman he'd fallen in love with was a prostitute. Billy pushed Crystal from under him before starting up the SUV and throwing it into gear before peeling off. She'd never seen him act this way, so she stared straight ahead as he sped toward town. She wondered how Billy was going to act once they got home, but the thought alone made her nervous. Billy still hadn't said a word, so she kept quiet as he drove over the speed limit more than halfway back to Vegas. She didn't have a clue what Billy was thinking because he wasn't driving in the direction toward Summerlin. She didn't know where they were headed, but she deeply regretted telling him about her past. They'd just been laughing and having an open discussion, so she thought that he'd be able to handle it. Just minutes before that, he'd said that he loved her, so she thought that it would be okay for her to be honest with him. Obviously, she had been wrong and would be sure that she'd never make that mistake again, Crystal thought.

Billy still hadn't looked in her direction since he'd learned that she'd been a prostitute. He believed that he loved her, but at the moment, he felt nothing but hatred toward her.

After pulling into the parking lot, Crystal realized what was happening. Instead of taking her back to his home in Summerlin, Billy had brought her back to the Budget Suites. He pulled directly in front of her room and stopped the SUV without saying a word. Crystal quickly hopped out and slammed the door behind her. As Billy sped off, she stood, indecisive about what to do, because not only does she have clothes and other belongings at Billy's house, but she still had the keys to the house and the BMW on her key ring.

Crystal stepped inside the quiet room and felt lonelier than she had in a long time. She became extremely dizzy, but this time, Billy wasn't by her side. Crystal stumbled a few times while trying to find her way to the bed. When she reached it, she fell heavily on top of it without realizing that she'd fallen. Crystal lay fully dressed across the bed, and she sobbed heavily until she fell asleep.

Chapter 22

Early the following morning, Billy sat at his desk sipping a cup of the hot coffee that Simone had already prepared by the time he'd arrived at the office. He sat with both feet kicked up on his desk with his eyes closed while thinking about Crystal. He didn't know how long it was going to take, but his mind was set on forgetting about her. Billy felt that Crystal had betrayed him by not telling him about her past in the beginning of their relationship. In the midst of his thoughts, he was suddenly startled by Simone's voice as it came blaring over the intercom. "Mr. Brocks, Mrs. Russell is here to see you, but I can't find where she's made an appointment."

"That's who I'm expecting, Simone. Send her in, please," Billy replied.

When the door swung open to Billy's office, he was shocked by the woman's beauty. Mrs. Russell had hired him almost a year earlier to get a divorce from her abusive husband. He'd seen her on a prior occasion, but couldn't recall her being so stunning.

Linda Russell was a very attractive woman in her late thirties, but appeared to be much younger. Standing six feet tall with a beautiful face and strawberry blonde hair reaching the center of her back, Billy was speechless.

As soon as she'd entered his office, Billy could smell her expensive perfume almost immediately. She strolled seductively across the carpet, wearing a tight pink dress that revealed every curve of her slim body. "Hello, Billy."

"Hello, Linda. It's good to see you again," Billy replied. "Here, have a seat."

"Thank you," she said as she sat down.

After a brief moment of silence, Billy Brocks spoke again, "Okay, Mrs. Russell, let's get down to business," he said while gathering some papers in front of him. "As of today, your divorce is final, and I'm going to read to you the settlement that both parties have stipulated to," he said while handing her a copy. "I'm explaining everything that you've won, but if you have any questions, please don't hesitate to ask me, okay?"

"Okay."

"I'm starting from the top, so you can read along with me if you'd like. Okay, you've been awarded the right to continue using the name Russell as your legal and correct name. The four-bedroom house located in Spanish Trails has been awarded to you. You've been awarded sole custody of your daughter so there won't be any custody battle. Mr. Russell has agreed to pay a sum of one thousand five hundred dollars per month in child support plus an additional half-million dollars in alimony. However, Mr. Russell has been awarded the right to keep all of his assets, including the yacht that he keeps at Lake Mead. Now with all of that being said, do you have any questions or comments?" he asked while staring at Linda.

"Billy, the only thing that I want to say is thank you for a wonderful job," she said with tears in her eyes.

Linda Russell was finally free. She felt that she had been trapped in a nightmare for five years, and it had finally come to an end. She was now free to raise her three-year-old daughter and move on with her life. Billy was looking forward to adding up everything he'd won for Ms. Russell and subtracting his 30 percent.

Linda Russell stood up from her chair before walking around to the other side of Billy's desk. As soon as he stood from his chair, she wrapped her arms tightly around him. "Thank you for everything," she whispered.

"No problem, Linda. Anytime," Billy replied while holding her tightly.

"I'm glad you feel like that because now that I'm divorced, you should allow me to cook dinner for you sometime," she said softly in his ear.

"That would be nice, Linda, but my schedule would probably make it nearly impossible," he explained while releasing her from his arms.

Linda gave Billy her cell phone number before kissing the paper she'd written it on. "Call me when you're ready," she said in a sweet voice.

"I'll do that," Billy replied.

Linda held both sides of Billy's face and boldly kissed him on the lips before leaving the office. He watched closely as she swayed her hips back and forth with every step. Before shutting the door behind her, Linda gave Billy a wink before blowing him a kiss. He knew at that moment that he had to have her.

Immediately after Linda's exit, Simone buzzed in on the intercom. "Mr. Brocks, a woman by the name of Crystal Tradwell has called several times. I told her that you were with a client, but she kept insisting on talking to you," she said in frustration.

"If she calls again, tell her I'm not here," Billy said calmly.

After seeing the sophisticated Linda Russell, Billy had forgotten all about Crystal. *Maybe if I took Linda up on that offer, I'll forget about Crystal for good,* Billy thought.

In the back of his mind, he already knew that, that's exactly what he would do.

Chapter 23

Crystal stormed out of her room at the Budget Suites, slamming the door behind her. She was upset because she'd called Billy's office several times, but his secretary kept saying that he was out in the field and that she didn't know when he would be back. Crystal was on her way to a nearby hotel to catch a cab to Billy's downtown office, but changed her mind immediately after she'd begun walking.

Once she'd made it back to her room, she headed straight to the telephone and tried calling Billy at his office again; but just like before, his secretary said that he hadn't made it back yet.

Crystal then called Angel at home and made arrangements to be picked up for work that evening. The two girls talked briefly; and although Crystal hadn't said anything about her and Billy's breakup, Angel knew that something was wrong, so she told Crystal that she'd be over as soon as possible so they could talk. After hanging up the phone with Angel, Crystal dialed another number. "Lickety Splits. This is Monica speaking. May I help you?"

"Hi, Monica, this is Crystal Tradwell. Is Barry in?"

"Hold on a minute," Monica said without waiting for a reply.

After holding for a few minutes, Crystal finally heard a familiar voice on the line. "Barry speaking."

"Oh hi, Barry."

"Hello there. Your voice sounds familiar, but I can't quite place it."

"Barry, it's Crystal."

"Oh hi, Crystal. How are you, sweetie?"

"I'm fine, Barry. I'm calling to see if it's okay for me to come back to work tonight?"

"Sure, sweetheart, I was beginning to wonder if you were ever coming back," he said jokingly.

"I know, it's been a while, but I've been trying to get myself well," Crystal said.

"Can you be here at eight o'clock?"

"I can be there at seven," she said with a giggle.

"See you tonight, and don't be late," Barry said before hanging up.

After taking a hot shower and preparing her clothes for the evening, Crystal drank all three beers that she had in the refrigerator. She got very relaxed as she stretched out on the couch and tried watching television for a while.

At five o'clock that evening, she was very tempted to call Billy at home, but decided against it since he hadn't called her. She was still in deep thought when she heard a knock on her room door. The knock was very familiar, so she already knew who it was before opening the door. When she pulled it open, she immediately began smiling while stretching out her arms to hug Angel. "Hey, girl," Angel said smiling.

"What's up, girl?" Crystal replied while moving aside and allowing Angel to enter.

"It's been a while since I've been over here," Angel said while looking around.

"Yes, it has, and you know I miss you," Crystal replied.

"So what happened between you and Billy?" Angel asked.

"He tripped out on me."

"For what?"

"Girl, I gave his ass some head yesterday, and when I finished, he had the audacity to ask me how I got so good at it," Crystal explained.

"He couldn't handle it, huh?"

"Girl, he told me that he's a lawyer, so he can't be fallin' in love with no whores."

"You really liked him too, huh?"

"To be honest, I think I love him," Crystal replied.

After staring at her friend for a few moments, Angel felt the need to console Crystal. "Come here, girl."

The two girls embraced each other for a long time before either of them spoke. Crystal cried on Angel's shoulder as Angel softly caressed her back. "Damn, I miss you," Angel said softly.

"I miss you too," Crystal replied.

"So you're that good at oral, huh?" Angel asked while sucking Crystal's earlobe.

"That's what I've heard," Crystal replied.

After holding each other tightly, Angel released her grip before kissing Crystal softly on the lips. Crystal responded by opening her mouth and allowing Angel's tongue to taste hers. She let out a soft moan while gently sucking Angel's tongue and playing with her nipple with her thumb and index finger. Angel gripped Crystal's ass with both hands as they continued to kiss passionately. She pulled Crystal's body closer to hers after Crystal removed her shirt and bra. Soon after, both of their bras were off, so Crystal began to kiss her way down Angel's neck before sucking on her swollen nipple and caressing the other nipple with her fingers. Instead of going over to the couch like they had before, the two girls removed their pants and panties before lying down on the soft carpet. Crystal lay flat on her back with her legs open while Angel straddled her face. Angel moaned softly as Crystal licked eagerly on her clit. They'd definitely been right about her being good with her mouth. Angel thought before leaning forward to return the favor. The two girls orally satisfied each other until each had reached orgasm.

Afterward, the girls went to the bathroom to take a shower. They bathed each other thoroughly as Angel explained everything that Crystal had missed at the club. They both screamed with excitement when Angel said that Frank had recently asked her to marry him. "I haven't given him an answer yet, but I plan to give him one soon," Angel said anxiously.

After they'd finished their showers and dried off, the two girls applied lotion to each other's bodies before getting dressed and preparing to leave.

Inside Angel's Nissan Maxima, they turned up their favorite radio station and sang out loud as they headed to work.

Chapter 24

After engaging in a short conversation with Barry, Crystal found herself nervous about going back on stage. She felt good and her body was somewhat relaxed as she thought about the evening she'd spent with Angel. She giggled while remembering the pleasure she'd felt before she realized that her nervousness was gone. Before removing any of her scanty outfit, Crystal quickly scanned the crowd to see if Billy was there. She glanced at the VIP section and thought about the night that she'd given him his first lap dance. She could still remember the way that he'd looked at her while she danced seductively in front of him. They had just been together the day before, and she was missing him terribly already. She wondered where he was and if he was thinking about her.

After dancing to her second song, Crystal's mind was so focused on Billy that she'd almost forgot to pick up her money before walking off stage. She hadn't paid any attention to any of the customers, so she was very surprised to see that someone had actually thrown some money on stage for her.

At the end of the night, Angel waited for Crystal inside the dressing room the same way she had in the past; but after Crystal had gotten dressed, she said that she wouldn't be needing a ride home that night. "I have a stop to make, so I'll take a cab," Crystal said

"All right, girl. I'll see you later," Angel replied.

Angel wondered where Crystal was going but didn't bother asking her. She thought about following whichever cab Crystal got into but quickly decided against it. After a quick hug goodbye, the two girls parted ways after making plans to get-together the following day.

Once Crystal was inside the cab, she gave the driver the address to where she wanted to go. She rode quietly in the backseat while counting the tips she'd made that night. She was also thinking about Billy, and she knew that she'd fallen in love with him, so she had no plans of allowing him to get away so easily.

Fifteen minutes after she'd entered the cab, the cab driver pulled up in front of the address that Crystal had given him. "Nice home," he said after stopping the meter.

"Thank you. It's my boyfriend's," Crystal replied while handing him the cab fare plus a five-dollar tip.

She climbed out of the cab and closed the door after thanking the driver. She noticed a white Escalade parked in Billy's driveway that didn't look familiar to her. She tried to recognize the vehicle while searching her purse for the house key that Billy had given her. After finding the key, she entered the home quietly. Although there weren't any lights on, she thought she heard what sounded like a television coming from upstairs. While walking through the kitchen, Crystal noticed some dirty dishes and empty wine bottles on the dining room table. She could feel the anger building inside her as she tiptoed up the stairs and toward the master bedroom. She wondered whom Billy had dinner with since she already knew that it hadn't been her. After turning the knob on the bedroom door, Crystal couldn't believe her eyes. Although Billy appeared to be asleep, a beautiful blonde woman lay in bed next to him staring directly at her. The woman had been watching television, but she and Billy were both lying there stark naked on top of the covers. "What is this?" Crystal yelled.

"Who are you?" the woman asked while shaking Billy awake. "Billy, who is this woman?" she asked in a scared voice.

Billy quickly rolled over and looked behind him. "Crystal, what are you doing here?"

"No, Billy, who the fuck is she, and why is she here?"

"Her name is Linda, and it's nothing for you to get upset about," Billy pleaded while climbing out of bed and putting on his pants.

"Billy, we were just together yesterday. I see it didn't take you long to find somebody else to sleep with," Crystal said with tears rolling down her face.

Billy walked over and gently wrapped his arm around Crystal. Although he was still upset about the day before, he had really begun to miss Crystal, and Linda Russell had been nowhere in comparison when it came to satisfying his needs. No woman had ever done that as well as Crystal, and he'd been thinking about her the entire time that he and Linda were being intimate. "Linda, I'm sorry, but I only allowed you to come over tonight because I was trying to forget about her," Billy explained.

Linda gathered her belongings as quickly as possible. She couldn't believe that things had turned out the way they had on the very day that her divorce was finalized. Crystal was still holding Billy close when Linda squeezed past them before bolting down the stairs and toward the front door. "I miss you, babe," Billy whispered.

"I miss you too," Crystal replied softly.

They had soon forgotten all about Linda as they held each other closely before making love for several hours.

Billy woke up about an hour before he would have to be at work. Crystal was still asleep but was quickly awakened when he entered her from the back. He decided to make love to her again before taking his shower. After climaxing, Billy kept his manhood inside her warm hole until slipping out. "We can't let that happen again," Crystal said suddenly.

"What?" Billy asked.

"Us breaking up."

"I know, sweetheart, and I apologize for getting upset about your past," Billy said before kissing her softly.

"Those days are over, and I only did it to survive," Crystal said before continuing. "You can never call me a whore again, Billy."

"I won't call you a whore, and I've already said that I'm sorry."

"I want you to promise me, regardless of what I do, you'll never call me that again," Crystal demanded.

"I promise, babe."

Crystal wasn't sure how much she believed Billy, but she was sure that she'd figure out a way to test him. She was glad to be back in his arms again, and she'd already forgiven him for sleeping with Linda. She thought about telling him about her and Angel but quickly decided against it.

After he'd taken his shower and gotten dressed for work, Billy stopped to give Crystal a kiss on the forehead. "I'll call you later," he said softly.

"I'll be here," she replied.

Although Crystal was happy to be back with Billy, she wasn't feeling too well. She'd gotten dizzy again, so she lay across the large bed and cried until she passed out.

Chapter 25

Several hours after being at his office, Billy remembered that he was supposed to check in with the Parole and Probation office. He thought about sending a fax but decided on calling instead. After finding the number in the white pages of the local phone book, he picked up the receiver and dialed quickly before reclining in his chair. "Parole and Probation, will you hold, please?" a woman asked.

"Yes, I'll hold," he replied.

Billy had been extremely busy the entire morning. He'd been preparing a brief that he'd hoped to have finished and filed by the end of the day. He really didn't have time to be left on hold for too long, so he grew restless after only a few minutes. He now understood how some of his own clients must feel after calling his office and being put on hold by Simone before talking to him. He was on the verge of hanging up when the woman came back on the line. "Thank you for holding. How can I help you?"

"My name is Billy Brocks, and I'm calling because I was told by the court to check in with this office to find out the name of my probation officer," Billy explained.

"You're that attorney, aren't you?" the woman asked with excitement.

"Yes, I am, and I know that I screwed up," Billy replied.

"Mr. Brocks, I don't know who your probation officer is going to be, but I'm sure they'll be reasonable enough to understand that you're a busy man. I'll make a note that you called, and I'll tell whoever it turns out to be that they need to contact you once the paperwork is processed," she said before continuing. "That way, you won't have to keep calling and asking who he or she is."

"That's very kind of you, ma'am," Billy said nicely.

"It sometimes takes a few weeks for the paperwork to be processed, but since you called, give it a few weeks to see if someone contacts you. If no one does, call me back and I'll look into it for you," the woman said.

"Who should I ask for when I call back?"

"Oh, I'm sorry, my name is Shanae."

"Okay, Shanae, I'll do that."

"All right, Mr. Brocks, thank you for calling and have a nice day."

"Same to you, Shanae," he said before hanging up.

Billy felt a lot better after talking to the woman at P and P. He turned his attention back to his desk where papers were scattered everywhere. He tried organizing the papers that would be filed until he was interrupted by Simone on the intercom. "Mr. Brocks, a woman just entered the office and walked right past me when I asked who she was," Simone said angrily.

"It's okay, Simone. I'll take care of it," Billy replied after seeing Crystal.

Crystal had already burst into Billy's office and hadn't bothered closing the door behind her. Billy watched closely as she strolled toward his desk wearing a facial expression that he'd never seen before. He became nervous because Crystal hadn't spoken or smiled since entering his office. She walked around his desk and pulled out his chair just enough for her to crawl into the space underneath it. After getting on her hands and knees and crawling into the small space, she pulled the chair forward with Billy still sitting inside. He didn't know what to do when she quickly unzipped his pants and pulled his limp manhood through the zipper hole. She covered his manhood with her mouth and gently began sucking it until it became fully erect. Billy couldn't allow himself to moan, so he shut his eyes and clenched his teeth tightly while Crystal performed fellatio. She continued to bob her head up and down until he'd reached orgasm.

After her brave performance, Crystal thoroughly cleaned Billy's manhood with her tongue before placing it back inside his pants. Without saying a word, she pushed his chair back and crawled from underneath the large desk. She climbed to her feet and exited the office just as quickly as she'd entered. When Billy opened his eyes, the first person he saw was Simone. She had been standing inside the doorway staring at him the entire time. Billy was so embarrassed that his entire face had turned red, and he found himself speechless. Simone didn't know what to say after witnessing the sex act. She held back her laughter because she knew that Billy was already embarrassed by what she'd seen. She simply pulled the door closed and allowed him to pull himself together.

After returning to her desk, Simone sat erectly while replaying the event in her mind. Although she's a very attractive woman herself, she hadn't been with a man for quite sometime. The episode with Billy had turned her on more than she'd realized, so she squeezed her legs tightly together in a desperate attempt to cool down the fire that she felt between them.

Chapter 26

Brocks & Brocks Law Offices were closing for the evening. Billy glanced at his watch while he and Simone exited the front door. They hadn't planned to walk each other out to their cars, but since they'd always parked next to each other, it's something they found themselves doing often.

While easing along the narrow sidewalk, Simone laughed out loud as she thought about the crazy afternoon she'd just experienced. "You have to be the luckiest lawyer in the world, Billy," she said with laughter.

"I didn't expect her to do that," Billy replied.

"C'mon. Don't tell me you didn't enjoy it."

"I'm not saying that I didn't enjoy it. I'd rather not even talk about it."

"I'm sorry," Simone said sincerely.

After reaching the parking lot, Simone and Billy said their good-byes as always. Simone got inside her two-seater Lexus and started the engine immediately. Before pulling off, she rolled down her passenger side window and called for Billy's attention. He had just opened the door on his SUV before glancing over his shoulder at Simone. She was inside her car pointing toward the smoky gray BMW that was also inside the firm's parking lot. As Billy turned to look in the direction that she was pointing, she burst out laughing before pulling off. Billy smiled when he saw Crystal sitting on the trunk of the BMW. She wore a long black skirt with slits going past her knees on both sides. Billy shut the door on the SUV before strolling over to where Crystal was parked. They both wore huge smiles as he approached the BMW. "Do you think I'm a whore now?" Crystal asked seductively.

"No, but I do think that you might be a little crazy," he answered while leaning forward to kiss her on the lips.

"If I'm crazy, I'm only crazy about you," Crystal said while pulling him between her legs.

Billy glanced around the half-empty parking lot. It would be considered unethical for him to be caught making out anywhere around the firm's property. He tried pulling Crystal off the trunk, but she resisted. "C'mon, Billy," she said while pulling him closer.

Once Billy stood between her legs, she raised her skirt so he'd see that she wasn't wearing any panties. "Give it to me, Billy! Right here, right now," Crystal said through clenched teeth.

"Are you crazy? We can't do it right here in front of the firm," Billy said in a serious voice.

"I went back to work last night, and I'll be there again tonight, so if we can't do it in front of your job, then we'll do it in front of mine," Crystal said angrily before hopping off the trunk of the BMW. She immediately got inside the car and pulled off while Billy stood in disbelief. He ran toward his SUV with the intention of catching Crystal, but she was long gone by the time he'd climbed inside.

When Billy arrived home, he was surprised to see that Crystal hadn't made it there yet. After waiting for a few minutes, he realized that she wasn't going to show up. He figured that she was just playing one of her little games, so he'd have to play along with her. He decided that he'd show up at Lickety Splits later on that night and give Crystal exactly what she wanted.

Chapter 27

It was almost midnight, and Billy still found himself sitting in the VIP section at Lickety Splits. He was confused because he'd been there since nine o'clock and still hadn't seen Crystal.

In the past, Crystal had been one of the first dancers to perform, but for some reason, she still hadn't come on stage yet. Billy had already seen his BMW parked outside when he arrived, but he still began to wonder if Crystal was even there.

While sitting in deep thought, he was suddenly interrupted by a man over the club's microphone. "Ladies and Gentleman, this is your last dance for the evening. It should be a real treat, so we hope you all enjoy."

At that moment, the lights inside the club were turned off before the colorful array of stage lights came on. Crystal slowly made her entrance to center stage and began dancing very seductively. She slid her crotch up and down a brass pole before bending over and allowing the crowd to watch as she removed her hot pink G-string. The crowd yelled with excitement as she caressed her swollen nipples with both hands while licking them at the same time. Crystal got down on all fours and began crawling as if leaving the stage until Angel appeared. Angel walked on stage and watched as Crystal crawled toward her. As soon as she'd reached Angel's feet, Crystal grabbed a hold of them and used Angel's body to climb to her own feet. Once standing, the two girls began kissing passionately while Angel squeezed Crystal's ass with both hands. Billy was in a trance as he watched the two girls kissing. The sight of them kissing had brought him to the edge of his seat as he continued to stare in disbelief. Seeing Crystal with another woman had really turned Billy on, and he found himself enjoying every minute of it.

Crystal had been giving him one surprise after another, and Billy wondered what he could do to surprise her. Angel and Crystal were just ending their sexual performance when the colorful stage lights went off. Everyone began to clap after seeing the heated performance, and they hadn't wanted to see it end so soon. Everyone stood up at the same time, so Billy had to force his way toward the front door as everyone moved into the aisles. He was anxious to see Crystal after witnessing her performance with Angel, and he didn't want to wait any longer than he had to.

Once outside the club, Billy was shocked because Crystal was already sitting on the trunk of the BMW. She was wearing the same black skirt that she'd worn earlier that day. As soon as Billy reached the car, he stood between Crystal's legs and began kissing her just as passionately as Angel had kissed her on stage. "Does this mean you still don't think I'm a whore?" Crystal asked as Billy slid her body to the edge of the car's trunk.

"I think you're gorgeous," Billy replied while fumbling with his zipper.

After taking out his manhood, Billy stared into Crystal's eyes before pushing himself deeply inside of her. He didn't care that people were still around and watching them, his only concern was to give Crystal what she wanted. He soon became lost in thought as he continued to make love to Crystal in the parking lot of Lickety Splits. Billy knew that he loved Crystal, so he blurted out the first thing that came to his mind. "Will you marry me, Crystal?" he asked before realizing what he'd said.

Crystal didn't know how to respond to Billy's proposal because she wasn't sure if he'd really meant it or if he was just in the heat of passion. He continued to thrust forward while awaiting Crystal's answer. "Yes, baby, I'll marry you," she said between breaths.

Billy laughed out loud as he continued to pump between Crystal's legs. He saw that she looked frightened, so he glanced over his shoulder in the direction that she was looking before noticing that someone was approaching them. "Knock it off!" the man yelled. "This kind of activity does not happen on my property, especially with my employees, Crystal. The rule book clearly states that it's automatic termination if something like this ever happened. Obviously, you don't care or you haven't taken the time to read the rulebook. You can come back tomorrow to pick up your money, but you can't work here anymore. I'm sorry," Barry said before turning to leave.

Crystal couldn't believe her ears. She wasn't sure how to feel because she'd never been fired from a job before. Billy had just proposed to her moments earlier, now Barry had just fired her. "Don't worry about it, babe," Billy said while zipping his pants.

“What do you mean don’t worry about it? You just got me fired!” she yelled angrily.

“What? You can’t be serious!” Billy replied.

He’d hoped that Crystal was only joking because she looked extremely serious. She reached inside of her purse and searched for the car keys without saying a word. She’d done the same thing earlier that day, so Billy turned and headed for his SUV just in case she was planning to evade him the way she’d done earlier. Crystal got inside the BMW and quickly started the engine before speeding out of the parking lot. Billy was already inside his SUV and was on her trail immediately after she’d made her exit. They were both in deep thought about the events that had just taken place, and Crystal smiled to herself as she envisioned herself in a long white wedding gown. Unfortunately, her happiness was short lived because her thoughts were suddenly overcame by extreme dizziness.

Chapter 28

Billy wiped his tears as Crystal went through the CAT scanner. He'd been told by a nurse to wait inside the waiting area and someone would come out to provide him with information as soon as it became available. Billy was baffled because he'd only looked away for a few seconds before hearing the loud crash. The light was red as he and Crystal approached it, but she'd failed to stop or slow down as they neared it. He didn't recall seeing the break lights light up on the BMW, so Billy wondered if Crystal had even seen the red light. The BMW had been completely totaled during the collision, but he wasn't worried at all about the car. He was more concerned about Crystal's physical condition. He had just asked her to marry him minutes before the accident, now he found himself waiting inside the same hospital that they'd come to when Crystal collapsed at work.

Crystal hadn't responded at all when he'd approached the car after the crash, so Billy knew that her injuries were serious. The paramedics had quickly arrived on the scene, so Billy followed closely behind as they rushed Crystal to the emergency room.

Dr. Chaps had been the same doctor who'd treated Crystal the first time they'd come to the hospital, so Billy recognized him immediately after he'd entered the waiting room. He assumed that the doctor was looking for him, so he quickly stood and approached him. "Is she okay, Doc?" he asked nervously.

"Well, she is awake. And as far as I can tell from the CAT scan, everything seems to be fine, so she should have a quick recovery. However, we won't know everything until all of the test results come back, but we do know that she's about six weeks pregnant," the doctor said while looking at Billy.

"What? Oh my god!" Billy said in disbelief.

"I take it you didn't know?"

"No, sir, we didn't know. Oh my god! When can I see her?"

"You should be allowed to see her shortly, and congratulations on the new baby," Dr. Chaps said before turning to leave.

"Thanks, Doc," Billy replied.

Shortly afterward, Billy was allowed inside Crystal's room. He walked all the way up to her bed before she looked up to see him. "I don't know what happened, babe. I got dizzy again."

"Don't worry about it, sweetheart. The doctor said you'll be fine."

"You talked to him already?"

"You mean they haven't talked to you?"

"They haven't told me anything."

"Babe, the doctor said that you're six weeks pregnant."

"What? Are you serious?"

"Yes, babe, we're having a baby."

"Maybe that's why I've been getting sick?"

"You'll be okay now, so don't worry about it," Billy assured her.

"What happened to the car?" she asked suddenly.

"The car isn't important, babe. Let's just worry about you for now," Billy replied while rubbing her head.

The nurse entered the room and basically relayed the same information that Dr. Chaps had already given. She said that the CAT scan had not revealed any internal injuries, but they wouldn't be certain until they receive the test results back. She also informed Crystal that they would be holding her at the hospital overnight for observation and advised her to get some rest before telling Billy that he only had a few more minutes left for visiting.

Shortly afterward, Billy and Crystal said their good-byes. He leaned forward and kissed her on the forehead before leaving the room. It was two thirty in the morning, and Billy had to be at work in about five hours. He decided he'd go home to rest his eyes for a few hours before going to work.

The drive home seemed like forever as he thought about Crystal and how the BMW looked after being rammed by the other car. It had been a terrible accident, and Crystal was lucky to have escaped it alive, he thought.

Billy was proud of himself because he and Crystal were now engaged to be married plus they had a baby to look forward to. Nothing else in the world seemed to matter. Crystal had simply come along and changed his life forever, and his only goal now was to make her happy in return.

When Billy arrived at his Summerlin home, everything seemed so different. He was so used to Crystal being by his side that, now that she wasn't there, he really missed her presence. Billy felt so alone, and the only thing that he could think about was his and Crystal's future together.

Chapter 29

At the hospital, Crystal was still trying to remember what had happened. Her neck was a little sore from the accident, but she knows that it could have been much worse.

Lying in the hospital was something that a lot of people dreaded, but Crystal was enjoying the time out. She found it to be very relaxing and a perfect time to think about her future

Regardless of all the bright lights, the lack of privacy, and the constant chaos that surrounded her, Crystal was proud of how dramatically her life had changed since leaving Atlanta. Things were happening so fast that they seemed unreal. A few months earlier, she'd been on the streets selling her precious body just to have enough money for food and shelter. Now she was close to fulfilling her dream of having the family that she'd always wanted and being as happy as she felt she deserved.

Defense attorney Billy Brocks had asked for her hand in marriage, and Crystal proudly accepted with no hesitation. Soon afterward, she'd learned that she was pregnant with his child, and she couldn't have asked for a better future.

The story seemed like a fairytale to Crystal as she rethought the events that had just taken place. The fact that she'd just been fired from the only job she's ever had and is now stretched out in a hospital bed resulting from a car accident, the story was reality and Crystal found herself looking forward to watching the drama unfold.

Although she had agreed to marry Billy, they had not yet set a date, so Crystal made a mental note to bring it to Billy's attention. She wanted to make arrangements to stroll down the aisle as soon as possible, and she hoped that Billy would feel the same way.

Chapter 30

Billy left his home at eight o'clock heading for work. The morning air was a little cold, so he immediately regretted not taking out the few minutes that it would have taken to prepare a cup of espresso. He climbed inside his SUV and traveled the same route he'd always traveled to get to work, but something was odd. Although everything looked the same, something felt different. *Maybe it's because I'm expecting a child and is engaged to be married*, Billy thought. The thought alone forced him to think about Crystal and how beautiful she'd looked even after the car accident. With her smooth golden skin, black curly hair, and almond-shaped eyes, Billy wondered who their child would favor most. He'd been in such a hurry to get dressed for work that he'd forgotten to call the hospital to check on Crystal's condition.

Still exhausted from all the events that had taken place the night before, Billy wasn't sure how long he'd be able to stay at the office that morning. It was Thursday, so there really wasn't that much work that needed to be done. A few briefs had already been prepared, so all Simone would have to do is run down to the courthouse and have them filed.

When Billy arrived at the office, he was delighted to smell the strong aroma of freshly brewed coffee that Simone had made. After pouring himself a cup, he happily accepted a glazed pastry that Simone had just removed from the microwave.

Once inside his office, he closed the door before calling the hospital to check on Crystal's condition. He was happy to learn that her health was fine, and she'd be discharged from the hospital as soon as he could leave the office to pick her up.

Immediately after the phone call, Billy called Simone into his office. He explained everything that happened the night before, and Simone was shocked. She had just recently met Crystal for the first time, now she learned that the young woman had been involved in a terrible accident. She gave Billy a warm hug and congratulated him after learning that he's an expectant father who's now engaged to be married. Simone was still smiling when she heard someone enter the office behind her. She immediately turned around to see who their guest was. "Hi, I'm Simone, Mr. Brocks's secretary. Is there something I can help you with?"

"Yes, my name is Jackie Proddy, and I'm here to see Mr. Brocks."

"Ma'am, maybe you should have called and made an appointment before coming to the office," Simone said nicely.

"I'm sure that that's probably the procedure for everyone else, but I'm Mr. Brocks's probation officer."

"Oh, I'm sorry, we weren't expecting you."

"That's the point of a surprise visit," the woman said rudely.

Simone informed Billy over the intercom that his probation officer was there to see him. Billy immediately came to his office door and invited the woman inside.

Jackie Proddy was a well-built woman who appeared to be in her late forties or early fifties. She dangled her small briefcase while entering Billy's office, so he pulled out a chair before gesturing for her to sit down. "I take it that my phone call to Parole and Probation is what brought you here?" Billy asked nervously.

"I did receive a message just yesterday that I should contact you as soon as possible," the woman replied.

"Well, it's good to finally meet you."

"And it's nice to see you again, Billy."

"Have we met before?"

"We have, but it was so long ago that you wouldn't remember. My name is Jackie Proddy, and I knew your mother when you were just a baby."

"You knew my mother?" Billy asked in an alarmed voice.

"I'm not here to talk about the past, Mr. Brocks. I just wanted to come over to introduce myself and make you aware of who your probation officer is; but yes, I did know your mother, and I'm sure she would be so proud of you."

Ms. Proddy noticed the look on Billy's face before deciding that it was time for her to leave. She stood and adjusted her skirt, and after shaking Billy's hand, she quickly made her exit.

Billy sat quietly at his desk. He was very confused and couldn't believe what he'd just heard. His father had rarely ever spoken of his mother, only to say that she'd run off and left soon after he was born. He suddenly remembered that he had to pick Crystal up from the hospital, so he walked out of his office, shutting the door behind him. He strolled over to the coffee machine and poured himself another cup. As the hot liquid emptied into his cup, he glanced at Simone. "Something very strange just happened, Simone. Ms. Proddy said that she knew my mother when I was a baby. That's weird because I've never had a mother," he said before leaving the office.

Since the weather had gotten a lot warmer than it had been earlier that morning, Billy rolled down all the windows on his SUV. From the time he'd climbed the freeway ramp until the time he made his exit, he thought about the visit he'd received from Jackie Proddy. He couldn't recall ever meeting anyone by that name, so he was quite sure that the woman had made a mistake.

After reaching Crystal's bedside, Billy was so happy to see her. He kissed her softly on the lips as she ran her hand over the top of his head. Crystal had missed Billy terribly that night, and she was glad that he'd finally shown up to get her.

Dr. Chaps had already given the nurse authorization to release Crystal from the hospital once Billy arrived. He'd also written a prescription for Crystal sometime during the night, so the nurse had it filled by the hospital's pharmacy and was ready to go by the time Billy arrived. Since Crystal was pregnant, Dr. Chaps had prescribed a special formula of vitamins to help abate her dizzy spells. He'd also given her an eight-month supply of prenatal vitamins free of charge. Crystal was told that her test results wouldn't be back until the following week, so the nurse informed her that the hospital would contact her as soon as the results were concluded.

After leaving the hospital, Billy helped Crystal as she climbed inside the SUV. He drove with extreme caution as he thought about the terrible accident he'd witnessed the night before.

While driving down the Las Vegas Strip, Crystal was surprised when Billy pulled into the parking lot of the Budget Suites. He parked directly in front of her room before instructing her to pack up all of her belongings. After entering the room, he straightened up as much as he could while she gathered her things. After they'd loaded everything inside the truck, Billy stopped at the front office and returned Crystal's room key. He also paid the fifty-dollar cleaning fee for whatever additional cleaning that they'd need to do.

After climbing back inside the truck, Billy leaned over and gave Crystal a kiss before heading for his home in Summerlin. While driving the backstreets, he expressed his undying love for her and assured her that she'd be well taken care of and would never have to do anything demeaning to survive again.

Chapter 31

Friday morning, Billy entered the building of Brocks & Brocks. Instead of taking the elevator, he decided on climbing the single flight of stairs to get to his second-floor office. When he reached the second floor, he spoke to a few attorneys that he passed along the hallway. After entering his office, he knew immediately that something was wrong. Simone sat expressionless at her desk while two black men dressed in expensive suits sat quietly on the leather sofa with their eyes fixed firmly on him. Billy stopped in his tracks and glanced back and forth between Simone and the two expensively dressed men. He was trying to figure out what was going on when both men stood and approached him. "Are you Billy Brocks?"

"Yes, I am. What can I help you guys with?"

"Mr. Brocks, my name is Malcolm and this is my partner, Corey. We're from the Bar Association, and we've been given the assignment of delivering this notice to you. If you'd like, you can sit down while you read it."

"No, I'll be fine," Billy replied while opening the envelope.

As he removed a single sheet of paper from the envelope, he braced himself as he unfolded it and began reading.

Dear Mr. Brocks,

The Bar Association has conducted a thorough investigation of your criminal conduct. Upon the completion of our investigation, we have concluded that you have violated your oath to a point that's irreparable. The board of the Bar Association has voted unanimously against you,

> *therefore, disbarring you as an attorney. Your license to practice law is hereby revoked, and a fine in the amount of five thousand dollars will be charged against your account. You'll have seven days to vacate your office at Brocks & Brocks.*

After reading the letter, Billy was speechless. His heart was pounding twice its normal speed before he realized that he'd needed to sit down after all. "Mr. Brocks, do you have any questions about what you've just read?"

"No, I understand fully," Billy replied while trembling.

"Okay, Mr. Brocks. We're very sorry that all of this has happened, but we do have a job to do, so we will be back in seven days to make sure that your office has been vacated," the taller of the two men said before turning to leave.

Billy stared at the two men as they left his office. He then looked over his shoulder at Simone before noticing the tears that streamed down both sides of her face. Without saying a word, Billy stood from his chair, picked up his briefcase, walked around Simone's desk and stood by her side. He put his arm around her shoulder and kissed her softly on top of the head before pulling away and exiting the office. Simone sat at her desk in disbelief and watched Billy leave the office for the first time as a nonlawyer.

Crystal was just getting out of the shower when she heard the phone ring. She wrapped the towel around her head so her hair could dry before running out of the bathroom naked to answer the phone that sat on the nightstand. "Hello."

"Hi, babe."

"Hey, honey, is something wrong?"

"Why do you ask that?"

"Your voice sounds like something is wrong. Are you at the office?"

"No, I just left the office. A couple of guys from the Bar Association was waiting for me when I showed up this morning. They gave me an envelope with a letter saying that I've been disbarred for my criminal conduct, and I have seven days to leave my office. Then to make matters worse, they gave me a five-thousand-dollar fine."

"What? Tell me you're joking."

"Why would I joke about something like this?"

"Is there anything you can do?"

"I haven't even thought about it yet. I don't know what to do or think anymore."

"Where are you now?"

"I'm in my truck. I'm calling because I need to sort through all of this, and I'm not sure what time I'll be home."

"Well, where are—" That was all she could say before he'd hung up.

Crystal was confused. *Does that mean he's not a lawyer anymore?* she asked herself.

She'd turned around and was headed toward the bathroom when the phone rang again. Thinking that Billy was calling back, she immediately turned around and ran toward it. "Hello."

"Hi, I'm calling to speak with Crystal Tradwell."

"This is she."

"Hi, Crystal, this is Dr. Chaps. Your test results came back a lot sooner than I expected, and I wanted to call you personally to let you know that it's very important that you come down to the hospital."

"Come down when?"

"Today, if possible."

"Well, it probably won't be today because something important is going on at home, and I need to be right here."

"Crystal, this is very important, and I really need to discuss these test results with you."

"If it's that important, you can tell me right now."

"It's against the hospital's policy to reveal test results over the phone. Our patient's privacy is very important to us, so we believe in confidentiality. If it'll make things easier for you, with your permission, I can mail the results to you."

"Yes, that'll be much easier."

"Okay, Crystal. I'll see to it that they're put in the mailbox today, and I hope to meet with you again soon.

"All right, Dr. Chaps. Thank you and I'll talk to you later."

After hanging up the phone with her doctor, Crystal called Billy's office. Simone answered the phone and confirmed what he'd already told her. After hanging up with Simone, Crystal rushed to get dressed. Her body had dried off completely while standing naked on the telephone. She had no place to go, but with the speed and energy she'd used getting dressed, one would have thought that she was running late for something.

After getting dressed, she brushed her long black hair with one hand while dialing Billy's cell phone number with the other. The recording indicated that the called party was unavailable, so she hung up and dialed again. For some reason, Crystal was nervous. She didn't know Billy's whereabouts, and he hadn't bothered calling home again. Crystal had not yet eaten breakfast, so she fixed a bowl of cold cereal and ate it quickly. Her hands trembled and she found herself staring at the kitchen phone, hoping Billy would call again.

After eating her cereal, Crystal ingested her daily intake of the vitamins that Dr. Chaps prescribed for her. She wondered what he'd wanted to discuss that was so important but quickly dismissed the thought as her mind returned to Billy. She entered the spacious living room and opened the drapes before pacing back and forth. Her mind was racing, so she glanced occasionally outside the large living room window to see if Billy's SUV had pulled into the driveway. It had been over an hour since he'd called, so she tried calling his cell phone again; but still, there was no answer. She tried calling the office again, but this time, Simone didn't answer. After several more failed attempts, Crystal had grown extremely frustrated. Billy wasn't answering his cell phone, and Simone was no longer at the office. She grabbed the remote control and turned on the television. After flipping through the channels, she sat on the couch and settled on a soap opera. After watching television for an hour, she got sleepy, so she kicked off her shoes and stretched out across the couch. Before she knew it, she'd shut her eyes and dozed off. Soon after falling asleep, Crystal was awakened by the sound of a slamming door. She glanced up just in time to catch Billy as he walked past the living room window. She was tempted to get up and open the door, but since he hadn't called her back, she stayed on the couch and allowed him to open the door himself. As soon as he entered the house, he saw Crystal sprawled out on the couch. "Oh hi, sweetheart."

"Don't hi-sweetheart me. Where the fuck were you, and why was your phone turned off?"

"Damn, what the hell are you mad at? Did you just get disbarred too?" he asked in a slurred voice.

"Billy, are you drunk? I smell alcohol all over you."

"I stopped at the bar and had a few drinks, but no, I'm not drunk."

Crystal grabbed Billy softly and cradled his head on her shoulder. "What are we going to do, honey?" she asked softly.

"I don't know, babe. I don't know," he whispered.

The two sat in silence for a few minutes before Crystal spoke again, "Maybe we should find something to do. Something that'll help us forget about what's going on."

"And what would that be?" Billy asked.

"I don't know, but I'm sure if we got out of this house, we could easily find something to get into."

After making the statement, Crystal slipped her feet back into her shoes before standing up. She pulled Billy to his feet and proceeded to pull him toward the front door.

At the hospital, Dr. Chaps sat quietly at his desk. He'd just finished addressing the envelope that he'd be using to mail Crystal's test results. He really wanted to speak with her in person about what the tests revealed, and after writing her name and address on the envelope, he wondered if he should just go over to the Summerlin address and pay her a visit after his shift ended. In midthought, his pager went off, and he learned that one of his elderly patients had just suffered a heart attack. Before rushing to the emergency room, Dr. Chaps quickly licked the envelope and sealed it before dropping it into the outgoing mailbox.

By midevening, Billy had forgotten all about the news he'd received from the Bar Association. He and Crystal had gone to the Strip and had brunch at one of Bally's most exquisite restaurants. Billy's good friend, Rosie, who's employed at the megaresort had given him several complimentary coupons to do different things if he ever found himself visiting the casino.

After filling their bellies, Billy and Crystal strolled up and down the Las Vegas Strip while stopping and taking chances at gambling in several of the Strip's casinos. They'd consumed a countless amount of free alcohol just for gambling at the casinos, which were all part of their plan. When they returned home that night, Crystal found herself hoping that her alcohol consumption wouldn't harm her unborn fetus. She quickly dismissed the thought when Billy pulled her into his arms and began kissing her passionately. The two lovebirds stripped down naked and made love on the living room floor, where they would both end up sleeping for the night.

Chapter 32

At seven o'clock Saturday morning, Crystal and Billy were awakened by a knock at the front door. They both lay naked with their clothes strewn all across the living room floor. While Billy checked to see who it was, Crystal quickly scrambled to gather their clothing. "Who is it?" Billy asked.

"It's Simone."

"Hold on, Simone. Give me a minute."

Billy was on his way upstairs to go to his bedroom when Crystal met him halfway with his bathrobe. She had also slipped into her robe, so she raised his bathrobe and held it open while he slipped his arms through the holes. Billy wrapped the robe tightly around his body before tying the belt to hold it together. He then walked back to the front door and proceeded to let Simone inside. "Good morning. Sorry to keep you waiting, but we weren't exactly expecting company."

"I'm sorry to intrude like this, Billy, but there's something very important that we need to talk about," Simone said while looking around.

"What is it?" Billy asked while locking the door.

"Well, I haven't really told you everything about me, and it seems like all that's been happening lately has started to make certain things make sense that never really made sense before."

"Things like what?"

"Billy, before you hired me as your secretary, I was dating this guy named Xavier. We were involved in a very serious relationship, and we even discussed marriage. But after you hired me to work for you, Xavier suddenly broke up with me. I didn't understand it at first, but he called me last night and explained everything. I don't know why it hadn't clicked in my mind, but Xavier is Philip Doolittle's son. It appears that there's always been bad blood between your family and theirs. Xavier is under the impression that your father had something to do with his mother's disappearance, which of course is Philip's wife. Your grandfather supposedly used his influence or something, according to what Philip told Xavier, to make sure that your father was never charged with anything. The history between the Doolittles and your family is not a good one. Billy, they hate you. That's why those comments were directed at you in court, and Xavier only broke up with me because I was working for you."

"Are you sure about all of this?"

"I'm telling you what Xavier told me. This thing goes a lot deeper than just you, and it may be enough to prove that you were intentionally provoked to act the way you did in court that morning. Not only that, but has it ever occurred to you that this incident took place in front of Judge Oram, and it just happens to be Judge Oram who sentences you? Isn't that a conflict of interest or something? There's just too many coincidences here, and I think you should at least look into it," Simone said before realizing the familiar smell. "Have you been drinking again, Billy?"

"No, Crystal and I went out last night to enjoy an evening together, and we had a few drinks," he said while smiling. "I really appreciate you stopping by, Simone; but I've been hit with one thing after another lately, and I kind of need a break. I will look into all of this and see if I can sort it all out. If I need you, I'll give you a call."

"Good luck with everything and be careful."

"Will do, Simone. Will do," he replied while closing the door behind her.

Crystal was shocked. She hadn't said a word the entire time Simone had been talking, but as soon as the door shut, she opened her mouth. "What the fuck is going on around here?"

"I don't know, but I'll try my best to find out," Billy replied. He was feeling hung over when he'd woke up; but after hearing what Simone had to say, he was now fully awake, so he squeezed past Crystal and headed upstairs for the bathroom. Billy's mind raced in all directions as he whipped out his penis and emptied his bladder. He then jumped in the shower and began to strategize. He pondered a while about what his first move should be until a thought occurred to him.

After drying off and wrapping a large towel around his waist, Billy went inside his bedroom to retrieve his telephone book. Once he'd found the number he was looking for, he sat on the front edge of his bed, removed the phone from the receiver, and dialed the number. After the phone rang several times, a muffled voice finally answered, "Hello."

"May I speak with Michael Shoemaker please?"

"Speaking."

"Good morning, Mike. This is Billy."

"Billy Brocks?"

"Yeah, Billy Brocks. Listen, Mike. I'm sorry for calling and disturbing you so early on a Saturday morning, but something very disturbing has been brought to my attention. I'm not even sure if you can help me out or not, but I'm wondering if you could answer a few questions for me?"

"Sure. What is it, Billy?"

"Mike, when you were hired way back when to take care of my father's legal affairs, what exactly was he accused of?"

"Well, if my memory serves me correctly, your father was never charged with anything."

"I didn't ask what he was charged with, I asked what the accusations was against him."

"I can't answer that, Billy, you know that."

"Why not?"

"You're an attorney, Billy. You know I'll always be bound by the attorney-client privilege of ever discussing your father's legal matters."

"I guess you haven't heard the news that I've been disbarred?"

"What?"

"Yep, they disbarred me; and I suspect a conspiracy, that's why I'm calling you."

"What does questions about your father have to do with what's going on with you?"

"I think some of the same people are involved that was around when my father was being accused of whatever it was he was being accused of."

"Involved in what, Billy?"

"I can't get into that right now, Mike. I understand you not being able to answer my questions, but can you at least tell me if it was my grandfather who'd hired you to represent my father?"

"I believe so. I think it was your grandfather who'd hired me."

"Thanks a lot, Mike. I'll get in touch if I need you," Billy said before hanging up.

Michael Shoemaker had not given Billy much help at all, so his mind continued to run rapidly. He walked to his walk-in closet and began getting dressed. He'd come up with another idea and decided to go check it out.

Crystal stood inside the bedroom's doorway and watched as Billy got dressed. "Can I go with you?"

"I need to be alone right now, honey. I'll take my bike and leave you the truck in case you need to go somewhere."

"I'll go see Angel. I haven't seen or talked to her in a while anyway."

"Drive carefully and make sure you eat something."

"All right, baby. I'll see you later," she said as Billy walked down the stairs toward the front door.

Billy was in deep thought as he swerved in and out of traffic on his customized Harley Davidson. He felt a little lightheaded when he stopped at a traffic light, so he decided to stop at Starbucks for a cup of coffee and a pastry before starting his day. He was in no rush. As an attorney, it seemed that he'd always had a certain time to do something. Whether it was watching the clock or the calendar, he was always on a time limit. For the first time since he could remember, Billy Brocks could finally take his time; but even now, his mind couldn't seem to slow down.

After arriving at Starbucks, Billy ordered his usual—a large cup of black coffee and a glazed pastry. Normally, he'd eat his snack on his way to work, but today was completely different. He no longer had a job, and he wasn't driving his truck, so he took a seat outside on the patio in front of Starbucks and enjoyed his breakfast while watching the traffic. For a Saturday morning, the traffic seemed a lot heavier than usual. The weather was nice, and the sun shined directly into his eyes as he tilted his head backward to take the last sip of his coffee. He tossed a crumpled napkin along with his empty coffee cup into a nearby trash bin before putting on his helmet. Although he did feel a lot better, he still felt a little lightheaded, but he didn't let it stop him from doing what he needed to do. Billy hopped on his bike and pulled out of the Starbucks parking lot before throttling the Harley quickly down the street. He wanted so desperately to find out if Simone's information was accurate. It was the weekend, so a lot of places might be closed until Monday, but Billy had a couple of places in mind. He turned the large Harley on Bonanza Boulevard and proceeded toward the west side of town. He sped up the long street, and soon after crossing Martin Luther King Boulevard, he turned into the parking lot of a publishing company. After parking his bike near the entrance, he removed his helmet and entered the building. After locating the editor's office, Billy noticed that the sign hanging in the center of the door didn't include a name. It simply read Chief Editor, so he entered the office and approached the only desk that sat inside. An older gentleman sat behind the desk with his eyes glued to a newspaper. He was a wise-looking man with salt-and-pepper hair wearing a pair of reading glasses that rested on the bridge of his nose. "Excuse me, sir. Are you the editor?" Billy asked.

"Didn't you read the sign on the door?"

"Yes, I did; but I didn't see a name, sir."

"You didn't ask my name, you asked if I was the editor.

"Yes, I see your point. Sir, I'm here because I'm wondering if you could help me out with something."

"It all depends on what you need, Billy."

"Did I miss something? I never said that my name was Billy."

"You didn't have to. I take it you haven't seen today's paper?"

"No, I haven't."

"You're on the cover. Here, check it out," the man said while folding the newspaper before turning it around so Billy could see it.

Billy stared at his picture on the front page of the Saturday newspaper. The headline only consisted of one word, which was in bold black print. Directly above his photograph was the word *DISBARRED*. Without saying a word, Billy snatched the newspaper off the editor's desk and began reading the article. It was only a few paragraphs, but it outlined his assault on the district attorney. It also explained that the Bar Association had notified him in person on Friday. The article said nothing about the information that Simone provided earlier that morning, so he immediately remembered his reason for coming to the editor's office. "Sir, you weren't even aware of today's paper, so it's obvious that you didn't come here to talk about it," the man said.

"No, this was just another surprise to me. I'm wondering if you guys keep all the back issues of the newspapers you've printed?"

"Sure, we do. Are you looking for a particular article on a particular day?"

"Well, actually, I'm interested in a particular time period. It could be several days, months, or even years. I really don't know yet."

"I would love to help you, but keep in mind that we print newspapers every day, so we have multiple volumes of back issues. It would be extremely time consuming if we tried to search through all the papers until we find the one or several that you're looking for."

"I completely understand that, but this is very important to me."

"Well, what exactly are you looking for?"

"I really don't know that either. Basically, anything I can find to support a theory that was recently brought to my attention."

"And what theory would that be?"

"I'd rather not say. Right now it's only hearsay."

"Billy, it's going to be very hard to help you if you don't help me."

"Sir, I'm here because somebody ran a theory past me. Now, if the theory is true, it would have been major news; and I'm sure it would have been printed in your newspaper."

"But you don't know the day, month, or year?"

"No, I don't, and it could be several dates."

"That's the problem. In order to find certain things, you'll have to know exactly what date it occurred. That way, I'll know which back issue or issues to dig up."

"I don't have that information, but I could try to find out more. I don't know about an exact date, but I could probably find out around what time or times these events occurred" Billy replied.

"Would you happen to know what these articles were about?"

"Like I said, it's only hearsay."

"Hearsay you don't care to repeat."

"That's correct. At least not at the moment."

"Would you happen to know who they're about?"

"Yes, I think I do," Billy said with confidence.

"Ahh, now we're getting somewhere. It seems that I'll be able to help you after all," the man said while smiling.

"How so?"

"Well, let me write down this address for you and I'll tell you. Go to this address and ask for Mary. She's a very good friend of mine, I mean a very good friend, if you know what I mean? Tell her Sammie sent you and she'll help you. I'll give her a call here myself in a few minutes, so she'll be expecting you. Tell her what you told me, and I'm sure she'll do what she can to help you. All you'll need to know is who the story was about," Sammie said as he handed Billy the paper with the address.

"Thanks a lot, Sammie. I really appreciate this," Billy replied after reviewing the address.

After leaving the editor's office, Billy walked swiftly as he headed toward the front exit. He strapped on his helmet, cranked up the engine, and throttled the large Harley down Bonanza Boulevard with more anticipation than ever.

Crystal left the house soon after Billy that morning. She didn't eat breakfast like he'd suggested, instead, she found herself pulling into the drive-thru of a nearby McDonalds.

After receiving her hotcakes and sausage, she realized she'd forgotten to order something to drink. She'd brought along her daily intake of vitamins that she planned to take after eating breakfast. She explained to the cashier that she had some vitamins that she needed to take, but she'd forgotten to order a beverage, so the young man looked over his shoulder before slipping her a free orange juice. "Because you're so beautiful, that's on the house," he said while smiling.

"Thank you, you're a real sweetheart," Crystal said before pulling away from the drive-thru window.

The morning traffic was busy, so Crystal took a couple of small bites from her breakfast while waiting to enter the main road. As soon as she'd spotted a gap between cars, she gripped the steering wheel with both hands and pressed firmly on the gas pedal. With several traffic lights along the way, Crystal took advantage of the opportunity. She'd eaten her entire breakfast and ingested her vitamins by the time she'd reached Angel's apartment complex. She drove the Yukon to the back end of the apartments and parked next to Angel's Nissan Maxima. She was very excited about seeing Angel because they hadn't seen each other since the time they'd danced together at Lickety Splits.

Crystal walked slowly up the walkway, adjusting the red sweater and white spandex skirt she is wearing. After reaching the door, she knocked softly with her keys. She heard footsteps approaching before the door swung open. "Hey, Crystal."

"Hey, Frank, what's up? Where my girl at?"

"Angel's not here. She went out of town for the weekend."

"Where she go?"

"She went to California to go shopping. You know how she do it."

"Yeah, I know she likes to dress. All right then, when she get back, tell her I stopped by," Crystal said while turning to leave.

"I'll let her know. Damn, girl! It look like that ass done got fatter," Frank said as she walked off.

"I'm a couple months pregnant, so it probably did," Crystal yelled back.

With no other plans in mind, Crystal decided she'd go back home. She didn't know when Billy would make it back, so she'd have to find something to do until he showed up. She had really hoped to see Angel, but that would have to wait until another time.

On her way home, Crystal pulled the SUV into the parking lot of a shopping center. She quickly found a parking space before going inside Blockbusters. After peering over several shelves, she finally picked out a couple of newly released DVDs that she wanted to watch.

Moments later, she was back inside the SUV, waiting for the opportunity to blend in with the rest of the heavy traffic.

While speeding down Rancho Drive, Crystal suddenly remembered the phone call that she received from Dr. Chaps the day before. Since she was already in the area, she decided to stop by the hospital to speak with him.

After reaching the hospital and finding somewhere to park, Crystal looked at herself in the rearview mirror before exiting the truck to go inside. She approached the counter and explained to a nurse that Dr. Chaps had called her the day before and asked that she come in to see him. The nurse confirmed the information before pointing Crystal down a hallway in the direction of Dr. Chaps's office. After reading the names inscribed on several of the doors, she finally found Dr. Chaps's office. As soon as she'd spotted his name on the wooden plaque, the door swung open. "Hi, Crystal. Come on in," Dr. Chaps said while clearing his throat.

"I was in the area so I decided to stop by."

"That's good. For a minute there, I was tempted to make a home visit. Well, like I said on the phone yesterday, this is a very important meeting; and there will be some important decisions you'll need to make," he said while closing the file cabinet after retrieving Crystal's file.

"What kind of decisions?"

"Well, decisions for you and your baby, I suppose. Here, see for yourself. These are all the results from the various tests that we conducted on the night of your car accident," he explained while opening the file in front of her.

Crystal looked at all of the papers closely. She scanned each page before glancing back up at Dr. Chaps. He stared back at her before speaking. "Do you see our problem?"

"I looked over everything, but I really don't understand all these medical terms," Crystal replied.

Dr. Chaps grabbed the file folder and began sifting through all the papers until he found the one he was looking for. He closed the file folder and placed the single sheet of paper on top of it before sitting it back in front of Crystal. "Don't worry about any of the other papers, this is the one we're mostly concerned with," he said while tapping the paper with his index finger.

Crystal reviewed the paper carefully. She looked over it several times, but still couldn't see what Dr. Chaps was talking about. "I'm looking at the paper, but I still don't understand what I'm suppose to be seeing."

"Did you read it, Crystal?"

"Yeah, I read it, but what am I suppose to be seeing?" she asked in frustration.

"It's self-explanatory. Are you in denial or are you really not understanding what it says?"

"I can't really read that good and the medical terms only make it harder."

"Crystal, this paper says that you've tested positive for acquired immune deficiency syndrome."

"What is that?"

"Oh my god, Crystal! This paper says that you have AIDS."

"AIDS! What are you talking about?"

"I'm sorry, Crystal, but that's what I've been trying to tell you. Now we need to start you on AZT and figure out what's best for your baby."

"Oh my god! Does that mean I'm dying?"

"We can't think about dying. Let's just focus on living and doing what's necessary to make sure you live as long as possible. I know it's tough, and I'm sure it's painful to hear, but you need to give me a list of everyone that you've slept with. Those individuals will need to be notified by our medical department and brought in for testing. You also need to tell your boyfriend right away so he can come down and get tested as well. Are you going to have a problem doing that, or should we notify him for you?"

"Oh no, I'll tell him. Please, let me tell him," Crystal begged.

"Okay, but I expect to see him in my office no later than next week. I saw him in the morning paper, so I know he's dealing with a lot already, but he still needs to know about this."

Crystal hadn't seen the morning paper, and at the moment, she wasn't the least bit concerned with it.

Dr. Chaps watched as Crystal daydreamed. *All that beauty is going to waste,* he thought to himself. "Well, Crystal, I know it's turned out to be a terrible day; but let me write a prescription to get you started on AZT, then you can be on your way. But make sure you get this filled as soon as possible," Dr. Chaps said while reaching for his ink pen. He scribbled the prescription and handed the order to Crystal after signing it. "I hope to see you early next week, and bring your boyfriend with you."

"He's my fiancé, and we'll be here," she replied sadly.

"Oh, your fiancé. Congratulations."

"Thank you."

Crystal walked quickly out of Dr. Chaps's office. He glanced quickly at her perfectly round ass as she left. *What a terrible waste,* he thought to himself.

Crystal walked briskly up the long hallway. Her world had suddenly been turned upside down, and all she could think about was Billy and the unborn fetus that was growing inside of her. Tears streamed uncontrollably down both sides of her face, so a lot of people were staring as she exited the hospital's front door. *How will I tell, Billy?* she asked herself. She had no idea how he'd handle the news, but she knew that she had to tell him.

Billy arrived at the address that Sammie had given him. He pulled his Harley into the parking lot before parking under a shade tree.

It was just past noon, and although the wind was blowing, the Las Vegas sun had already begun to heat up. Billy removed his helmet and wiped the sweat from his forehead with a napkin he'd stuffed in his pocket at Starbucks that morning. He felt relieved after entering the building. The cool air blowing from the air conditioner felt a lot better than the hot wind blowing outside. Billy looked around at all the computers that filled the room. They were in perfect order, and each one was separated by a divider, giving each computer ample space on each side to prevent one user from peeking over the shoulder of another. As he scanned the room, he noticed that a beautiful black woman was approaching him, so he turned and smiled when she got closer. "Hi, ma'am, I was told to ask for a lady named Mary. Would you happen to know who she is?" Billy asked.

"Yes, she's in her office. Follow this aisle to the end, and you'll see her office on the right hand side," the lady said while gesturing with her hand.

"Thanks a lot, ma'am."

"Lorene. My name is Lorene."

"Thanks, Lorene."

"You're welcome, sir."

Billy walked until he'd reached the end of the aisle, and just as Lorene had said, he immediately saw Mary's office on the right hand side. The door was slightly open, so he knocked softly before peering inside. "Oh, you must be Billy?" the lady asked after he'd peeked inside.

"Yes, I am. And you must be Mary because you wouldn't know my name if Sammie hadn't called you."

"That's not necessarily true. I also saw you in today's newspaper."

"Oh yeah, I forgot about that," Billy replied.

"Sammie did call me, but I'm still confused about the help you need. He tried explaining it to me, but obviously, he didn't do a very good job because I still need you to make it clear for me."

"Well, I'm looking for some information that was probably big news many years ago. I don't know exactly when it occurred, but Sammie said that you'll be able to help me if I knew the names of the people involved. Right now, it's no more than hearsay, so I'm trying to be reticent until I'm able to confirm something," Billy explained.

"I see. You're searching for something that happened in the past. And although you don't know exactly when it happened, you do know that is was big news or should have been big news, and you think that you know the people who was involved or people that you suspect were involved?"

"That's correct."

"All righty then, I'll tell you what I'll do. I'll pull out our multivolume directory. Any information that we have on file will be listed in the directory. The information we store stems back to the beginning of Las Vegas's history, all the way until now.

So if you don't find it in the directory, that means we don't have it on any of our files," Mary explained while walking toward the other end of the library.

After removing three large notebooks from the shelf, Mary handed the books to Billy while looking directly into his baby blue eyes. "These are the directories. Use whichever one's you need, but it's everything we have from A to Z. The last names of the people involved in any prior newspaper articles are all listed in alphabetical order. Once, or if you find what you're looking for, the directory will list a disk number. All disks from A to Z are located in that file drawer over there. Whichever disk number the directory gives you, get the disk from the file drawer and use one of these five computers back here because these are the only ones that's equipped with the disk drives that'll activate these nonmagnetic optical disks. However, you'll only be allowed to have one disk out at a time. Each disk will pull up the entire article or articles ever printed about the people you're looking for. In this basket over here, you'll find a couple of pencils and whatever scratch paper you may need to jot down information if you need to. If you have any additional questions, you can find me either in my office or at the front counter," Mary said before walking away.

"Thank you," Billy replied.

Immediately after Mary had left, Billy sat in one of the computer booths and opened the first directory. It began with the letter *A*, so he set the other two notebooks aside. He flipped through several of the *A* pages before reaching the *B*s. Once he'd reached the *B* section, he sat erect on his chair and searched until finding the *Br*s. There were several pages of *Br*s, so he flipped from one page to another until he saw his last name staring back at him. Billy jumped up quickly and ran to the basket that sat on top of a small file cabinet. He retrieved a pencil and a few sheets of scratch paper from the basket before returning to his seat. He quickly wrote down the page number that the name Brocks was on, and the disk number that was in the column next to it. The disk was filed under 52-H, so he went to the file drawer containing the disks and searched anxiously until finding the one he sought. He slid the disk quickly into the disk drive, typed in the name Brocks, gave the mouse a few clicks, and a list of dates appeared on the computer's monitor. The dates ranged between 1967 and 1969, so Billy decided he'd begin with the earliest. He used the mouse to direct the arrow toward 1967. After giving it a click, three different dates appeared on the screen. The dates were September 20, October 18, and November 24. He directed the arrow to September 20 and clicked the mouse. An article titled QUESTIONABLE CONDUCT appeared across the screen, so he began reading. He learned that his grandfather Edwin Brocks, Sr., had been suspected of bribing certain judges along with the chief of police in order to operate an illegal prostitution ring. No evidence had ever surfaced that could prove the allegations, so no arrests were ever made.

Billy guided the arrow to October 18 and read another headline: CRIMINALS WHO DEFEND CRIMINALS. This time he learned that his father Edwin Brocks, Jr., had been accused of having sex with an underaged prostitute, and Edwin Brocks, Sr., had retained none other than Michael Shoemaker out of San Francisco to defend the case if necessary. It turned out, charges were never filed against Edwin Brocks, Jr., because the underaged prostitute had mysteriously gone missing.

Billy was in shock. He took the arrow down to November 24, and after clicking the mouse, he stared at the screen in disbelief. The headline read, FEMALE OFFICER'S DISAPPEARANCE. Billy read the article and confirmed what Simone had told him earlier that morning. Officer Judy Doolittle had mysteriously disappeared after going undercover to pose as a teenage prostitute. Again, Edwin Brocks, Jr., was the prime suspect. The article explained that Judy and Philip Doolittle were newlyweds who'd just had their first child together. No charges were ever filed because the body of Judy Doolittle had never been found.

This information was too much for Billy. He felt drained, and a slight dizziness had come over him, but he continued to move forward.

He directed the arrow down to 1968 before clicking the mouse. Only two dates appeared for 1968, and both were for the month of February. On February 7, an article was printed on the father-son duo. Edwin Brocks, Sr., had been suspected of committing several white-collar crimes including money laundering, racketeering, extortion, pandering, and embezzlement. Edwin Brocks, Jr., was suspected of kidnapping, murder, and several counts of statutory rape. Charges had never been brought against either of the two attorneys. The article spoke briefly about the expansion of Brocks & Brocks, only to suggest that authorities lacked evidence to put the firm under investigation.

The next date Billy went for was February 13. The headline simply read, IS SHE SAFE? In the center of the article was Billy's father Edwin Brocks, Jr., along with a teenage girl. Billy learned that the young girl's name was Ruby. It turned out, Ruby was his older sister who'd been born out of wedlock. The article talked about Edwin Brocks, Jr., and his illegitimate daughter. Why didn't they tell me I had an older sister? Billy asked himself. He stared at the photograph and noticed the strong resemblance. Billy found himself wanting to go find his older sister. He had always been the only child, so it would have been nice to grow up with an older sibling, he thought.

He guided the arrow down to 1969 before clicking the mouse. This time, only one date appeared on the monitor. The date was August 20, so he immediately clicked the mouse to get to it. This headline read: SHOULD WE BLAME THE STATE? Billy's heart began beating fast and his throat had suddenly become dry as he tried swallowing. Ruby had disappeared, and rumors had spread that Edwin Brocks, Jr., was responsible. The article explained that the state was at fault for not removing Ruby from her father's custody. Ruby was reported to have been seen having cuts and bruises on her face by some of their neighbors on several occasions prior to her disappearance. She had also been removed from her public school after becoming pregnant at the age of thirteen, and she'd just given birth to a son about four months before her disappearance. The article gave no indication as to where the baby was now.

Billy could barely breathe. He was baffled by the information, but felt extremely angry toward his father and grandfather. What had happened to his sister and nephew? Billy wondered.

Without thinking, he was on his feet and heading in the direction of Mary's office. He was very upset, and his mind raced in all directions. He stopped suddenly when he saw the two women walking up the aisle in his direction. "Gosh, what happened?" Mary asked.

"I was just coming to look for you," he replied.

"Excuse me if I'm wrong, but judging by how red your face is, I assume that something is wrong?"

"Something is definitely wrong. I found far more than I was looking for, and I'm wondering if I could get a copy of what I've found?"

"I have a meeting to attend in a few minutes, but Lorene here will be happy to help you," Mary said while looking at Lorene.

"Thank you so much. I really appreciate this," Billy replied.

"Come show me what you need," Lorene said nicely.

After going back to the computer, Billy directed the arrow to the bottom of the screen before clicking the mouse. The index page appeared on the screen, so he explained that he wanted to copy all six articles printed about the Brocks's between 1967 and 1969. Some terrible things had taken place within that three-year radius, and Billy had plans of finding out more.

Lorene set up the printer, typed in the data, and pressed enter. Shortly afterward, Billy had his copies in hand. He removed the disk from the disk drive and stared at it before handing it to Lorene. "Thank you."

"No problem," she replied.

Billy turned toward the front entrance and strolled slowly up the aisle. Lorene watched as he walked away before turning to return the disk to the file drawer. She returned the disk to the slot 52-H and envisioned Billy's face as she closed the drawer. She didn't know for a fact, but she was pretty certain that she'd always associate that disk with Billy's face.

Billy placed the copies inside a black leather satchel that he'd kept under the seat of his Harley. He slung the bag over his shoulder and put on his helmet before mounting the large bike.

Once he'd gotten onto the main road, he gunned the bike forward as he headed home.

Crystal's heart began pounding harder as soon as she heard the Harley ride up the driveway. She'd been pacing around the house for several hours after returning home from the hospital. She was very upset at herself for allowing such a terrible thing to happen to her, but she knew that it was very important that she tell Billy about it.

After parking the Harley on the side of the house, Billy was greeted at the front door by a nervous Crystal. She gave him a hug and a peck on the cheek after he'd entered the house and shut the door behind him. "Hi, babe. How was your day?" she asked nervously.

"It was terrible," Billy replied while slipping the satchel over his head.

"Mine was terrible too, and I really need to talk to you about it."

"Babe, I'm beat. I'm sorry, but I just can't think straight right now. This had to be the worst day of my life, and I don't even know who I am anymore," Billy said while walking up the stairs.

Crystal was still standing by the front door. Unsure of what to do next, she went into the living room and turned on the television. Remembering the DVDs she'd rented, she headed upstairs toward their bedroom. Billy lay across the bed, reading what appeared to be photocopies of something. "Babe, I've rented a couple of comedy movies. You wanna watch 'em with me?" she asked seductively.

"No, Crystal! Dammit, I've already told you that I'm tired. I'm trying to read, so please, don't bother me anymore!" Billy yelled.

Without another word, Crystal turned and headed back downstairs to the living room. Her feelings were severely hurt, so she cried as she sat down in front of the television.

A few hours later, Billy came downstairs and walked into the kitchen, grabbing a slice of left over pizza and a soda from the refrigerator before going back upstairs.

Crystal still sat in the living room, staring blankly at the TV screen. The two would not see each other anymore that evening. Crystal fell asleep in the living room while Billy slept alone upstairs in the bedroom.

Chapter 33

Sunday morning, Billy found himself sitting at the bar of a nearby pool hall. He'd had a hard time sleeping and had woken up several times during the night.

After learning all he'd learned about his family at the library the day before, he was feeling sick. The information had simply been too much to handle all at once, so he thought he deserved a break. He still felt lightheaded and had begun experiencing mild dizzy spells, so he knew that his current hardships were beginning to take its toll.

Crystal was still asleep on the living room couch when he'd left home that morning. He found himself deeply regretting that he'd been so mean to her the night before, so he planned to make it up to her as soon as he got home from the pool hall. If he could ever figure out a way to deal with his family's past, he would explain everything to Crystal; but since there's still a few things that he needs to find out, he has to wait until he has all the pieces to the complex puzzle before trying to put it all together. "Can I get you another drink?" the bartender asked.

"Yeah, make it a double," Billy replied.

Crystal sat at the kitchen table eating her breakfast. She'd learned that Billy was gone after going to the bedroom after waking up on the living room couch. She had no clue where he'd gone, so she decided she'd scramble herself a few eggs and take her medication before calling his cell phone. Crystal was in deep thought. She didn't understand how something like this could happen to her after finally getting her life together. After swallowing the last of her scrambled eggs, she felt a slight movement in her belly. She thought about her baby and wondered if it would be a boy or a girl.

After leaving the kitchen, Crystal headed upstairs. When she entered the bedroom, she saw Billy's cell phone sitting on the nightstand beside the bed. He had never left home without his phone, so she wondered if he'd left it on purpose. Remembering how he'd screamed at her the night before, she wondered if Billy was still upset with her. She noticed the small stack of photocopies that he was reading when he yelled at her. They were sitting on top of the black leather satchel, so she picked them up and began reading.

Although her reading was below average, she clearly understood Billy's pain. After reading and understanding as much as she could, Crystal sat on the edge of the bed. Her mouth dropped open as she learned what Billy had learned about his family. She really wished that she knew where he was at the moment because she felt an incredible urge to comfort him. She was standing right there when Simone explained the details of a telephone conversation she'd had with her ex-boyfriend. She'd said that the Doolittles hated Billy, and in one of the articles, there was proof that justified their feelings. She laid the articles back on top of the satchel in the exact order she'd found them. *With all of his current pressure, how could he ever handle the news I have for him?* Crystal asked herself. Her heart had gone out to Billy, and she hoped he'd hurry home so she could be by his side.

Chapter 34

At nine thirty Monday morning, Billy opened his eyes and found himself cradled in Crystal's arms. She was already awake and had been staring at his face ever since she'd awakened fifteen minutes earlier. "Good morning, honey," she said softly.

"Good morning, babe," he replied.

Billy was feeling nauseated. He was suffering from a severe hangover from all the drinking he'd done the day before, but he still knew he had something to do. He climbed out of bed after glancing at the clock, and although he felt terrible, he stretched and yawned before looking back at Crystal. "Babe, can you put on some coffee for me? I have a few things that I need to do, so I'll jump in the shower and see if I can wake up."

"Sure, I'll make some coffee and have something ready for you to eat when you finish showering."

"Thanks, sweetheart."

As Billy prepared for his shower, Crystal climbed out of bed and headed downstairs to the kitchen. She wondered when she'd get the chance to talk to Billy. He'd been so drunk when he got home the night before that she hadn't wasted her time trying to tell him anything. Besides, after reading the articles and learning what he'd learned about his family, she'd just wanted to be by his side to comfort him. She'd waited the entire night to tell him about her problem, and now that he was leaving again, she didn't know when she'd get the opportunity to speak with him.

After changing the coffee filter and refilling a new one with fresh coffee grounds, Crystal turned on the automatic coffeemaker. Afterward, she reached inside a cabinet and removed a frying pan to prepare Billy's breakfast.

A short time later, Billy came down the stairs, buttoning the sleeves on his shirt. He went directly to a bottom drawer and pulled out two large trash bags before sitting them on the floor in front of the front door. After sitting at the kitchen table, Crystal sat his breakfast in front of him. "Is this for me?" he asked jokingly.

"Who else would I be cooking for?" she replied while sitting his coffee in front of him.

"This is delicious," he said after swallowing a forkful.

"Thank you."

Once he'd finished his breakfast, Billy stood from the table, wiping his mouth with a napkin before looking down to make sure he hadn't spilled any food on his clothes. "Well, I'll be seeing you later," he said while leaning forward and kissing her on the cheek.

"All right, baby. Make sure you take your phone with you."

"I have it. I shouldn't be gone too long."

After picking up the trash bags he'd left on the floor, Billy went out the front door. Soon afterward, the large Yukon was backing out of the driveway.

When he arrived at the firm, Billy parked the truck in his usual parking space. He grabbed the trash bags that he'd laid in the passenger's seat and began walking toward the building. When he entered, he recognized a lot of familiar faces, but didn't bother speaking as he climbed the stairs to get to his second-floor office. The office was a lot quieter than he was used to, but he closed the door and began packing his things. For a moment, Billy wondered what Simone would do about finding another job; but remembering her strong ambition, he knew she'd be all right. He filled both trash bags with his personal belongings before looking around the spacious office. He was really going to miss the place, and he smiled to himself while thinking about the memories he'd made. While shutting the door to his office, Billy breathed a deep breath before walking over to Simone's desk. He picked up the phone and shut his eyes for a few seconds before dialing a number. "District Attorney's Office, Philip Doolittle speaking."

"Phil, this is Billy. I know you probably don't want to hear from me, but I wanted to apologize for everything that my family has ever done to hurt your family. I can't imagine the amount of hatred you must feel when you think about us, but after recently learning what you already know, I wanted to personally say that I'm sorry."

"This phone call is a total shock to me, Billy. After all these years, it's good to see that there's hope for a Brocks after all. Your apology is accepted, and thanks for calling."

"I don't know what to say to that, sir."

"You don't have to say anything. You've already said enough."

Billy felt a lot better after talking to Philip Doolittle. After hanging up the phone, he looked around the office once more before leaving for the last time. He carried both trash bags through the lobby as he headed toward the front door. After placing the bags on the backseat of his SUV, Billy's mind was not clear. He still had a couple of questions and was determined to have them answered. He drove to a location not far from Brocks & Brocks. After pulling into the parking lot and climbing from his truck, he entered the building through a side door. After stopping in the lobby and looking over a bulletin board, Billy headed toward the stairs. After reaching the second level, he inched his way down a hallway until finding the office he sought. As soon as he walked inside, an older woman with dyed red hair glanced up from behind a desk. She had been reading the Holy Bible, which she quickly put down when Billy walked inside the office. "Good morning, sir. How can I help you?"

"I'm here to see Jackie Proddy."

"Is she expecting you?"

"She's my probation officer. Is she in this morning?"

"Yes, she is. What is your name, sir?"

"Billy Brocks."

"Oh, I know who you are. I just read something about you in the newspaper this past weekend. I'll tell her you're here."

"I'd appreciate that."

After making a phone call, the lady hung up and looked at Billy. "You can go through that door right there. Ms. Proddy is expecting you."

"Thank you."

After entering the office, Billy closed the door behind him after seeing Jackie Proddy sitting on the corner of her desk. She wore a red skirt and a white blouse that clearly exposed her ample cleavage. "What brings you here?" she asked while uncrossing her thick legs.

"A few things," Billy replied.

"A few things like what?"

"Well, Ms. Proddy, over the weekend, I went to the library and learned many disturbing things about my family that I've never known about. When you visited my office, you mentioned knowing my mother when I was a baby, and I'm here to learn about that."

"Mr. Brocks, I don't want to get involved with your family affairs because it's none of my business."

"I understand that totally, but it's my business, and it's very important that I learn about my mother. I've learned about all the terrible things that my father and grandfather were suspected of, and they've only told me negative things about my mother. After learning what I have about them, I no longer trust anything that they've ever told me. For Christ's sake, I've even learned that I have an older sister and a nephew that I've never even known about. Did you ever meet my sister Ruby? According to law officials, she disappeared shortly after giving birth to my nephew," Billy said angrily.

After staring at the floor for what seemed like forever, Jackie Proddy looked up at him. Her eyes filled with tears that were soon rolling down both sides of her face. Billy stared at his probation officer intensely. He knew that he must have said something that struck a nerve in the attractive woman, so he remained quiet while waiting for her to speak. "Billy, I've spent most of my life trying to push back these terrible memories. I will explain the truth to you, but we must agree that you'll never come around here again after today. Seeing your face only makes things more difficult, so I'll allow you to serve out your probation without ever having to worry about either of us making contact. Is that a deal?"

"It's a deal."

After taking a few moments to compose herself, Jackie Proddy began to speak. "Okay, judging from the synopsis you just gave me, I can see that you still don't have all the facts. Everything you've said so far is true. Your father and grandfather were terrible, awful men. Everything they did was corrupt and extremely diabolical. Your mother was my childhood friend, and we attended the same school together. At the beginning of the seventh grade, she would always complain to me about the abuse she was suffering at home. She didn't appreciate the way that your father was treating her, and she was on the verge of reporting him to the authorities, but she feared he'd find out because of your grandfather's powerful influence. Back in those days, your grandfather owned several government officials. There were rumors that he was affiliated with the mob, but I can't say how true that is. I do know that he was untouchable by the law because most were on his payroll. That's why your father was never arrested or charged with anything after being the prime suspect in many of the young girls' deaths and disappearances. Soon after your mother had become pregnant, your father immediately took her out of school, and I've never had the privilege of seeing my friend again. Billy, the child that Ruby gave birth to was you. Your father turned to incest after the heat was turned up on all the cases where young prostitutes who'd either been killed or disappeared had gone unsolved. There was speculation that your father had probably learned of Ruby's plans of exposing him, so he got rid of her. But that was never proven."

By this time, Billy had heard enough. His face was covered in tears before he'd stood up to leave. He stormed out of Jackie Proddy's office and ran down the hallway holding his stomach. He ran down the stairs and out of the same door he'd come in through. When Billy reached his SUV, he threw up outside of the driver's side door because learning about his father's sickness, of incest, had made him sick to his stomach. He spat the remaining vomit from his mouth and climbed inside the Yukon. He'd been receiving one blow after another for the past few months, and he wasn't sure if he could take anymore. He now hated what he stood for and wished that he could somehow change it all.

Billy started the engine on the large truck, swung it into gear, and headed home. The only thing he wanted now was to feel Crystal's arms around him.

After arriving home, Billy was forced to wait in the middle of the street because the mailman was blocking his driveway with his mail truck. Immediately after he'd moved it, Billy pulled quickly into his driveway. He decided he'd wait until later before removing the trash bags that he'd used to clean out his office. After climbing from the SUV, Billy retrieved the mail from the mailbox. Once he'd entered the house, he climbed the stairs and headed toward his bedroom. The bathroom door was closed, but since the light was visible underneath and the shower was running, he headed back downstairs and sat on the living room couch. He decided to read the mail that he'd still been carrying while waiting for Crystal to finish showering. Most of it were junk mail, but he came across something that had been sent from the hospital. Although it was addressed to Crystal, he figured that it was her hospital bill, so he decided to open it. After unfolding the paper and glancing over it, Billy's entire body began to stiffen. He didn't know what to think as his world continued to cave in around him. His heart was pounding as if trying to jump out of his chest as he read over the paper again. He ran up the stairs, knocked on the bathroom door, and waited for Crystal to answer. "Crystal!" he yelled.

There was still no response, so he turned the doorknob and pushed the door open. "Crystal, are you in there?" He still didn't get an answer, so he peeked inside the shower curtain. "Oh my god, Crystal!" he yelled before snatching the curtain open and shutting off the water. Crystal lay at the bottom of the tub completely naked. Her body was half covered with soap as he pulled her up to a sitting position. "Crystal, talk to me, baby! Please talk to me! Oh god, please don't let this be happening!"

It didn't matter how many times Billy called out Crystal's name, she would never answer him again.

Chapter 35

A week after finding Crystal dead in the bathtub, Billy attended her funeral. He'd purchased a pretty white dress and had taken it down to the mortuary so that Crystal could look like an angel while lying in her all-white casket. Billy fought back his tears as he stood over Crystal's body. She looked extremely beautiful, and it appeared that she was only taking a nap. The coroner's report concluded that Crystal's cause of death had resulted from an advanced stage of the AIDS virus, and it was this information that troubled Billy. The funeral proceedings were kept short and simple. Billy was the only one to attend, so the pastor had been in and out of the church in twenty minutes or less.

Crystal was not from Las Vegas, so there weren't many people who knew her. The few that did know her were not aware that she'd passed because Billy wanted to keep things as nonchalant as possible. The past week had been pure hell for him, and all he'd done was mope around the house and watch his life go from bad to worse. In his thirty-four years of life, Crystal had been the only woman that he'd ever grown to love. She was the only woman who'd ever managed to find her way inside his heart and made him feel so complete. While gazing down at Crystal's face, Billy gave her a soft kiss on the cheek. "No matter what, I will always love you," he whispered before turning to leave.

Since no other family or friends had attended the funeral, the mortuary had provided their own pallbearers to carry the casket. Once the casket was placed inside the hearse, Billy jumped inside his SUV and followed it slowly to the cemetery.

After Crystal's body was laid to rest, Billy breathed a sigh of relief. He had paid his last respects and provided Crystal with a decent burial, so all he could do now was try to move on to see what the future held for him. He'd done a lot of thinking over the past week, and he decided that Las Vegas had simply ruined his life. It was time to relocate and try to enjoy whatever future he had left.

Chapter 36

Two years after Crystal's funeral, Billy Brocks had relocated. His Summerlin home had been sold to the highest bidder soon after he'd put it on the market, so he'd packed his bags and moved to Phoenix, Arizona. His days of living lavishly were over. Although he still drove the expensive Yukon, Billy had either sold or given away mostly all of his material possessions. His health was slowly declining, so he chose to spend the majority of his time either drinking or cruising Phoenix's South Side, searching for local prostitutes. His dizzy spells were occurring more often, and they seemed to be getting more severe each time they came. The symptoms were quite familiar, so he didn't need anyone to tell him what was happening.

On a cloudy morning, Billy left his apartment to buy groceries at a nearby grocery store. While pushing the grocery cart down the aisle, his vision suddenly blurred. He stopped and tried refocusing, but it only became worse. The lights had become extremely bright, and his legs became weak. The moment he'd attempted to reach out to grab hold of a shelf, he suddenly collapsed.

Several hours later, he woke up in the emergency room of a Phoenix hospital. He didn't know what had happened, so he began panicking when he saw all the tubes that had been inserted into his body. When he sat up and jerked the IV from his arm, a nurse yelled while rushing to his side. "We need a doctor!"

"What's going on? What's happening!" Billy yelled.

"I'll tell you in a minute, sir. First, let me reattach your IV," the nurse replied while moving quickly. "You were rushed here by the paramedics this morning, apparently, some witnesses inside a grocery store saw you collapse before passing out in the middle of the aisle."

"What are all these tubes for?"

"Hold on, here's your doctor. I'll let him explain," she said while moving aside.

"How you feeling, sir? I'm Dr. McCullough. Most of my patients just call me Dr. Mac, I guess, because it's easier."

"Doc, what are all these tubes for?" Billy repeated.

"Well, according to some witnesses, you fell out in the middle of a supermarket. Being a doctor, I know that as one of the known symptoms of a very serious disease. Not saying that something is wrong with you, but it's standard procedure for us doctors to take certain safety precautions in these types of situations."

"How long will I have to stay here?" Billy asked.

"It all depends. It's mandatory that I test you thoroughly. I understand you wanting to go home, but it would be malpractice on my part if I allowed you to leave the hospital without conducting these tests. We can have your results back later today or tomorrow at the latest. If you turn out to be sick, we can start you on the proper medication as soon as possible."

"Are you referring to AIDS?" Billy asked calmly.

"AIDS or HIV is what you're being tested for, yes. But like I explained, we're not saying you have it. But what happened to you in that grocery store this morning is definitely one of the many symptoms that doctors are aware of. These safety precautions will allow us to find out now and treat it at this stage so you'll still live a long and prosperous life if you are infected."

"So you're saying because I collapsed in that grocery store, not saying that I do, but you suspect that I could have AIDS?"

"That's correct."

"And every doctor should know that?"

"I really can't speak for the doctors in other countries, but in America, yes. It's knowledge that's repeated constantly throughout medical school."

"Thanks, Doc. I guess I'll just make myself at home."

After the doctor left his bedside, Billy took in a deep breath. He stared at all the tubes and the few machines that stood beeping around him before lying back on the bed. He sunk his head deeper into the pillow as his mind drifted to Crystal. He really missed her company, and tears rolled down each side of his face as he thought about what Dr. Mac had just told him. Crystal did not have to die, but the fact that she had only made him furious. He raised a hand to wipe the tears from his eyes while looking around. At that moment, he had already made up his mind to check himself out of the hospital.

Later that evening, Billy searched through some old files that he'd kept in a storage area of his apartment building. After finding the one he was looking for, he reviewed the file before picking up the telephone and dialed a number. "Hello."

"May I speak to Chuck, please?"

"Yes, hold on a minute."

After waiting for what seemed like forever, a man's voice came over the telephone. "Yeah."

"Is this Chuck?"

"Yeah, this is Chuck. Who is this?"

"It's Billy."

"Oh, what's up, Billy? I heard what went down, and I'm sorry to hear about you losing your license."

"I'm not worried about that. Hey, listen, it's important that we talk. Is there any way that we could do that in private?"

"Sounds serious."

"It's very serious, so how should we go about communicating?"

After discussing everything in a lingo that only they understood, Billy and Chuck reached an understanding. Billy hung up the phone and was overcome by a strong sense of power. To ease his mind, he decided that it was time he'd have a few drinks before searching for a lady of the evening. Although he hated to admit it, Billy couldn't deny the fact that the blood of his father and grandfather was running through him, and he'd began to think like them. After drinking a double shot of whiskey, he thought about which young prostitute he'd spend the night with.

Chapter 37

For a city that proclaimed to never sleep, Las Vegas seemed extremely calm except for the strong winds and heavy rain. Although the airports were still up and operating, a lot of flights had been canceled, and only a few remaining flights would be keeping their schedules to depart from McCarran Airport for other destinations. The next flight would be leaving for LAX at 8:15 p.m., which a lot of people were already in line and ready to aboard.

At 7:45 p.m., a large figure emerged from between two minivans that were parked inside a semifilled parking lot. The figure wore no more than surgeon's scrubs, a surgeon's mask, and a see-through raincoat that dripped with rain. As he approached the well-lit entrance of the building, a deafening sound of thunder roared loudly as a flash of lightening lit up the gloomy sky. When the sliding doors slid open, the figure entered the building with his head down while stomping his feet, as if making sure that all the water would be cleared from his black designer boots. He moved swiftly down a hallway and into an office before three muffled gunshots quickly rang out. After a man fell to the floor, the figure turned around and made his exit just as quickly as he'd entered.

Moments later, Dr. Chaps was found dead on the floor of his office, just as the assailant was boarding the eight-fifteen flight to Los Angeles.

The following morning, Billy Brocks was laid up in a motel room in downtown Phoenix when his cell phone rang. "Hello."

"Remember our last meeting when you said I owe you one?"

"I remember."

"We're even."

Although the call was extremely brief, Billy clearly understood the message that was given. As he stared at the young prostitute that he'd spent the night with, he suddenly recalled what his father and grandfather had always taught him: Don't ever trust women! Billy reminisced about all the wonderful times that he and Crystal had shared. When he closed his eyes, the last thought that crossed his mind was a question that he'd often asked himself, *What's next for you*? This time, Billy had an answer—*Death!*